# Somewhere
## BETWEEN

*To Sherrie,
Best always!
Patty Wiseman*

# PATTY WISEMAN

# Books by
# PATTY WISEMAN

**VELVET SHOE COLLECTION**
*An Unlikely Arrangement*
*An Unlikely Beginning*
*An Unlikely Conclusion*
*An Unlikely Deception*

*Success Your Way*

*That One Moment*

*Rescue At Wiseman's Pond*

*Somewhere Between*

1209 South Main Street
PMB 126
Lindale, Texas 75771

This book is a work of fiction. Therefore, all names, places, characters, and situations are a product of the author's imagination and used fictitiously. Any resemblance to actual persons, living or dead, places, or events is entirely coincidental.

Copyright © 2018 Patty Wiseman

All rights reserved. No part of this book may be used or reproduced in any manner whatsoever. For information address Book Liftoff 1209 South Main Street #126, Lindale, TX 75771.

Interior Book design by Champagne Book Design
Printed in the United States of America

Library of Congress Control Number Data
Wiseman, Patty
Somewhere Between / Patty Wiseman.
Historical—Romance—Fiction.2. Ghost—Romance—Fiction.
Fiction. | BISAC: FICTION / Romance / paranormal. | Fiction / Romance / Suspense.

Library of Congress 2018937569
First Edition.

ISBN: 978-1-947946-36-1

www.pattywiseman.com
www.bookliftoff.com

## *Praise for*
# SOMEWHERE BETWEEN

Patty Wiseman has masterfully devised a captivating tale. Her powerfully descriptive writing convincingly transports the reader to 1856 Texas. There, she skillfully peels away layer after layer of an intriguing and ever-intensifying mystery. Wiseman holds the reader spellbound, eager for what awaits on the next page. Patty effectively weaves the supernatural with the everyday, utilizing well-paced and enjoyable dialogue throughout. The various colorful subplots are neatly and deliciously wrapped up in a most gratifying conclusion.

—Mike Hawron, author.

# Dedication

To all those who found the courage to follow their dreams. To those who are looking for the courage to take a chance. To those who break the chains of self-doubt and spread their wings to soar the currents of a dream fulfilled, this book is dedicated to you!

"Find out who you are and do it on purpose."
~Dolly Parton

# Chapter ONE

*1856 Texas*

They call it Queens Court Acres. A prestigious name considering its ill-repair.

Phebe Whiteside stared at the imposing architecture, craned her neck to inspect the twin turrets above—and blinked. A face peered through a lace curtain from the sky-parlor above. She blinked again.

It was gone.

Imagination?

Not one to fall prey to illusions, she shook off the odd sensation and focused on the task at hand.

A lion's head brass knocker adorned the mammoth door, which she lifted and let drop. The reverberation echoed through the old house.

She waited.

A week ago, a letter of acceptance for the position of governess to the Powell's three children arrived by post. "A day for new beginnings," she sighed.

Most women her age were already married. Phebe's dreams, loftier than most, carried her in a different direction much to her parent's chagrin.

Mr. Whiteside, a printer by trade, found it difficult to say no to his golden-haired precocious daughter and gave permission sans his wife's approval.

At nineteen, she took employment with a prosperous family in the city and taught there until the children became adults.

Now thirty-seven, she was forced to start anew.

The door opened. A tall, very erect gentleman in a white linen coat, black tie, and gray trousers greeted her, his tone crisp, "Ms. Whiteside? My name is Winston. Come in. Mr. and Mrs. Powell await you in the study."

His voice suited the pinched, disapproving look on his face.

Her wide eyes took in the butler from the top of his white hair to the tip of his shiny black shoes. *He is a proper one.*

A quick wave and confident smile was all she gave her father as she stepped inside.

"Is that your father?" Winston asked.

"Yes."

"You don't want him to accompany you for the interview?"

"No, I can manage on my own."

The opulent foyer took her breath away. Elegance abounded with high ceilings, dark intricate woodwork, a sweeping staircase, and the focal point—a gleaming glass chandelier.

*Like stepping into a storybook.*

"No time to dawdle. This way." Winston pursed his lips, knit his eyebrows, and tapped an impatient foot on the black and white tile floor.

Air re-entered her lungs with a gasp. "Yes, pardon me. It's only…"

He swept across the room to another imposing door. "In here."

Her footsteps sounded like the rat-a-tat of a woodpecker as she hastened to catch up. She smoothed her rumpled gray skirt, removed her dark blue travel bonnet, and announced, "I'm ready."

His churlish demeanor softened, "Are you sure you don't want your father to accompany you?"

She squared her shoulders. "No need."

The perfunctory statement produced a tiny quiver at the corner of his mouth.

*A sign of his approval?*

His face returned to its former pugnacious mask. "As you wish." He opened the door. "May I present Ms. Phebe Whiteside."

Soft murmurs inside the room subsided.

The butler stepped aside and gestured she enter the room.

Large paned windows filtered the outside light and made it hard to see the faces of her employers.

She fluttered her eyelids until vision returned.

A stout, middle-aged man sat in a wingback chair behind a Cherrywood desk. His hair was dark brown, but thinning. A cigar rested between his fingers, unlit.

A slim woman perched on a chaise lounge next to a stone fireplace. "Welcome, Ms. Whiteside," she said.

Phebe curtseyed. "Thank you."

Emma Powell spoke again, "Please come closer so we can see you better."

She complied. "Yes, ma'am."

Phebe saw a hint of a smile on the pleasant, round face of Mrs. Powell, who sat straight with both hands in her lap. Faded blonde hair, tamed by a French twist, complimented the muted blue of her long dress with its high collar.

Charles Powell projected a more severe look. Black suit, no smile.

"Are you sure you can handle three lively children? I'm their mother and I find it difficult, at times."

"Why yes, I'm the youngest of seven siblings. The bustle of children, house-keeping, and cooking is normal in my household. And of course, there's my previous employment. Two lively boys for almost fifteen years."

The Powell's exchanged glances.

"You may be qualified at that," Mr. Powell smiled, transforming the dour look, revealing plump cheeks and a twinkle in his dark eyes. He flicked at the fallow cigar.

"We've gone through several governesses lately. They babble on about a noise in the attic. I hope you aren't scared off by a few rattling timbers in this old house." Mrs. Powell's bright blue eyes clouded; the smile disappeared.

"Creaking boards won't bother me."

Mr. Powell stood. "Good. The letter of recommendation from your parson and previous employer impressed us. We hope this arrangement works for all of us. Winston will show you to your quarters and introduce you to the children. You'll start promptly at seven in the morning in the children's breakfast room. Winston will give you the itinerary. Good day, Ms. Whiteside."

She curtseyed again. "Thank you."

Mrs. Powell rang a small china bell.

Winston appeared.

"Please show Ms. Whiteside her quarters and introduce her to the children with the schedule for the week." She turned back to Phebe. "A tray will be brought to your room for dinner. You should rest. Tomorrow's activities will, no doubt, tax your strength."

"Yes, ma'am. Oh, may I introduce you to my father, first? He's waiting in the carriage. It'll be a comfort for him to see I'm in good hands.

"Why yes, Mr. Powell and I would love to meet him. Winston, show him in please."

Winston nodded curtly and left.

A few minutes later, he ushered her father into the library.

"May I present Mr. Whiteside."

Mr. Powell came around the desk with hand extended. "Good to meet you, sir. We're pleased to welcome your daughter into our employ."

"She'll work hard and give you no trouble." Whiteside smiled and shook hands with vigor.

"No doubt. May we offer you a cup of tea?"

"No, thank you. I must go. My wife is poorly. I must attend her." He reached out to shake hands with Phebe. "Do us proud, my dear. Write when you can."

"Oh Papa!" She ignored the formal handshake and threw her arms around him. "I love you so much. Don't worry. Please tell mama I love her."

Whiteside cleared his throat and gently removed her arms. "Yes. Now, Phebe, you settle in and attend to your work. I'll be going." He wiped his eyes.

She remained in the study as he waved goodbye, her smile brave, but precarious. Life just changed again. Among strangers once more, she faltered and took a step forward.

Winston closed the door.

"He loves you very much, my dear," Mrs. Powell said softly.

Tears threatened to erode her well-crafted resolve. She could only nod at her new mistress.

Winston stepped forward. "This way, Ms. Phebe."

The slight moment of weakness waned at the kindness in his voice. She followed him down a narrow hall to the kitchen.

"This is the servant's access to the children's quarters." He looked back at her. "Be sure you use only this stairway, not the main one."

"Certainly." She followed him up the dark, wooden staircase and made a mental note to carry a candle during the night hours.

*I wonder if I'm allowed downstairs after dark. It might be a good idea to make a list of questions to ask. One does not upset pre-established protocol.* She smiled at her assessment of the situation. *I think I'll fit in exceptionally well in this household.*

A wide hallway opened at the landing. Identical ivory doors lined each side as far as she could see. The house, quite large from what she observed outside, came into perspective inside and revealed the true scope of its expanse.

*I hope I don't get lost up here.*

"The first door on the right is the breakfast room. The children always eat their first meal here. Lunch is on the veranda with their parents, if weather permits, otherwise they'll revert to this room. Dinner is served in the dining room with Mr. and Mrs. Powell, unless they're entertaining. Again, they'll eat here in that case." Winston stated the schedule of meals matter-of-factly, didn't repeat it, nor ask if she understood.

"Where are the children now?"

For a moment, she saw another crack in his armor. His eyes flickered, his lips parted. A fleeting look of fear crossed his countenance, but dissolved quickly.

"They're in the school room with Cook."

"She is teaching them?"

"There's been no one else since the last governess. Cook's twenty years with the Powell's left her no choice but to agree when they asked."

"Oh."

"The school room is at the end of the hall. Your bedroom and the children's rooms are in between. Would you like to see your room before you meet the children?"

"I'd love to meet the children first. I'm sure Cook will want to get back to the kitchen."

Winston nodded. "This way."

She passed each door and wondered which room was

hers, but excitement of meeting the children overruled curiosity.

He stopped at the last one on the left. Even in the hallway, chaos sounded through the classroom door. Children screaming, a woman's voice pleading for them to stop.

Winston squared his shoulders and opened the door.

Immediate silence greeted them.

Cook stood behind the teacher's desk trying to coax down a little girl of about five. One boy, older than the girl, tugged at Cook's skirt, screaming to let her alone. A second boy rifled through the teacher's desk. They froze like mannequins at a general store when the door opened.

Cook found her voice first, while tucking disheveled strands of white hair back under her cockeyed cap, face flushed like a young maiden. "Please tell me this is the new governess."

Winston gave his signature curt nod. "Yes, Ms. Phebe Whiteside."

The two boys rushed forward. The girl jumped from the desk and joined her brothers; all asking questions and tugging at her skirt.

Phebe nearly toppled over under the onslaught. "Wait, please, one at a time. Ladies first." She focused on the girl. "Tell me your name."

The girl gazed wide-eyed at Phebe. "Have you come to help us find the ghost?"

## Chapter TWO

"My name is Elizabet. I'm five." She crossed her arms and stamped her foot, raven black curls bouncing like springs. "I *said* are you gonna help us find the ghost?"

Winston clucked his tongue. "We'll not indulge in such talk on Ms. Phebe's first day."

Phebe diverted the attention to the oldest boy. "And your name?"

Sudden shyness cloaked the previously brazen child. His mud brown eyes grew wider. "Uh, my name?"

Phebe nodded.

"I'm Benjamin." He blushed.

She turned to the younger boy. "And you?"

A bastion of freckles exploded like fairy dust into a huge smile. "My name is Charley."

"Good. Everyone's called me Ms. Whiteside, but I say we start out on a different note. You may call me Ms. Phebe. Agreed?"

Elizabet tucked her chin with a scowl.

"Is something wrong, young lady?"

"You didn't answer me. I'm the only girl. You should answer me first."

She knelt next to the pouting child. "Well, where I come from, we give each other mutual respect. How rude would I be if I didn't address your brothers properly? There'll be plenty of time for questions. At bedtime, I'll come to each room and give you my undivided attention before you go to sleep. For now, back to lessons."

Winston and Cook exchanged surprised glances.

*Do they expect me to fail like the previous governesses? Father says I possess a gift when it comes to children. Come down to their level, demand respect, and never compromise your authority*

Elizabet, Benjamin, and Charley blinked like owls in the dark of night.

The children answered in unison, "Yes, Ms. Phebe."

They scampered to their desks, folded their hands, and remained quiet.

Cook stared, open mouthed, a Scottish brogue revealing her heritage. "Well, if that don't beat all. I've never in my born days seen them act so polite."

Winston gaped, as well.

"Glory be! It's that good to meet ya, Ms. Phebe. Maybe now I can keep to cookin'." Her head wagged back and forth as she hurried to administer a huge hug. "Never seen anything like it."

She returned the embrace. "I'm so happy to be here. And what might I call you?"

Cook straightened her apron. "Why, they call me Cook 'round here.

"No, I insist. If I'm to call Winston by his name, I certainly want to call you by yours. What is it?"

"It's Myrtle Godwin."

"Wonderful. Myrtle it is."

Myrtle blushed. "I'll let you all get back to it. Dinner won't prepare itself. Come down to the kitchen anytime. We'll get acquainted." The door closed behind her.

Winston stood rooted to the spot.

"Winston, let the children show me their rooms, then we can return to schooling."

"As you wish."

The children squealed and grabbed her hands.

"Ladies first boys. Elizabet will you please show me your bedroom?"

In orderly fashion, each child proudly escorted her to their respective rooms.

After each inspection and with appropriate glory and acclaim, she asked, "Now, where is mine?"

Benjamin volunteered. "I'll take you."

He stopped right next to Elizabet's.

Benjamin opened the door and gallantly swept his hand to invite her inside.

The room was beautiful. Sparse in its furnishings, but done in a subdued pink gingham fashion. It suited her.

She bent down and whispered to Elizabet. "We're right next to each other. It could be fun."

The little girl turned adoring olive-green eyes to her new governess. "Secrets without the boys? Girl secrets?"

Phebe nodded, watching the color, flecked with amber, dance in the child's eyes.

She studied the eyes of the boys to see if theirs matched Elizabet's, but neither quite measured up, instead they resembled mud puddles, no spark, no dazzle.

*Ah, she's a spitfire, for sure, with those eyes!*

She sighed. "Now, let's go back to the classroom. What were you studying when I interrupted?"

Charley frowned. "Cook tried to get us to read a book."

They led her back to the school room.

Winston's face softened, for an instant, no hint of a smile, but a definite diminishing of the ever-present pursed lips. "You've certainly worked magic on them. It seems they really like you."

His signature gruff manner returned quickly, the compressed lips once more in place. "Dinner is in an hour. The children will dine with their parents. You may take dinner in your room or with me and Cook in the kitchen. I'm sure you're exhausted, so it's fine if you'd rather enjoy a bit of solitude."

"I'd love to share a meal with you and Myrtle. You can tell me all about this ghost."

## Chapter THREE

Displeasure transformed Winston's face, eyes black with fury, lips white with anger at the mention of the ghost.

She decided to shrug off his churlish demeanor and finished the hour by reading a book with the children. They relished her suggestion of acting out each scene. Benjamin wanted the part of the bear. Charley wanted to be the wolf. Elizabet acted out the part of the princess. By the end, they collapsed in a heap, laughing. It was a grand time. She almost forgot about Winston's sinister reaction.

He came to escort them to dinner with their parents.

The children complained, reluctant to leave.

Phebe suggested, "Tell them of the book you read, act out your parts. It'll be a jolly conversation."

They scampered out of the room all talking at once.

In the kitchen, Myrtle applied the finishing touches on two large trays.

"Can I help?"

Myrtle smiled, her jolly face red from the heat of the kitchen. "Oh, goodness no. Winston always does the honors. You sit down. I'll serve ya the first course."

"No need, I can serve myself."

"Well, what a breath of fresh air you are!"

Winston returned and lifted the trays, balancing one on each hand in an experienced manner.

"He looks like he's done this forever."

"He has. Can't remember a time when he wasn't in this house."

"Ah, that reminds me. What of the ghost the children mentioned? Did you ever encounter such a thing?"

Myrtle glanced up. "I wouldn't be askin' about such things."

Phebe leaned closer. "And why not? Even the children think there's a ghost here? Where does it come from?"

"It's not an it. It's a 'he'. The previous owner of this estate."

She pulled up a stool, eager to hear all the details. "What's his name? Did he die here?"

"Edmund. Yes, he died here, murdered."

"Murdered?"

Myrtle sighed. "Well, no one knows for sure. He was found dead in the sky-parlor. The doctor couldn't determine a cause of death. Said his heart probably gave out. But, he was only twenty-four." She glanced around the kitchen as if a spy lurked about. She lowered her voice. "A rumor circulated. Poison."

"Poison? Who would do that?"

Myrtle's scowled. "Lordy, girl. You do ask a lot of questions."

"I love a good mystery and old houses, too. Why would someone poison him? Was he a vile man?"

"Well, there's the mystery. The only clue was a wine glass next to the body. No one knew what to make of it. He wasn't much of a drinker." Cook pointed the spoon at Phebe. "It's best you not bring it up. The Powell's don't take kindly to prying into family business."

Winston reappeared. "If you are talking about that silly ghost I'll take my meal elsewhere."

"I wouldn't dream of chasing you away, Winston. Myrtle caught me up on the story. The children ask about it, thought I might prepare a better answer for them."

Myrtle winked. "It's a sore spot with old Winston here. *He* wants to be the only mysterious male in the manor."

"Nonsense." He brushed off the feckless comment. "Let's change the subject. Are your accommodations satisfactory?"

"They're beautiful, thank you."

Myrtle placed a steaming plate of roast beef, carrots, potatoes, and a biscuit in front of her. "Eat up."

The savory aroma sparked her appetite. She dug in with gusto, banishing all thoughts of the ghost.

# Chapter FOUR

PHEBE VISITED THE CHILDREN'S ROOMS AT BEDTIME. Each child regaled her with their acting abilities, insisting *they* were the best actors at dinner. Reenactments followed, accompanied by her rapt attention. It wasn't long before they fell asleep exhausted from their new experiences.

The darkened hall brought the alleged ghost to mind as she padded softly toward her room. *Not one of them mentioned Edmund, which is unfortunate. Best I don't ask the children—but stick with Myrtle.*

Settled in her cozy bedchamber, she snuggled into the soft mattress, pulled the pink patchwork coverlet over her and opened a copy of *Moby Dick*, a present from her parents.

After reading several pages, her eyelids drooped. When the book fell to the floor, she extinguished the lamp and pulled the blankets to her chin. The silvery glow of the moon faintly illuminated the room, a soothing comfort.

She fell asleep satisfied with her first day.

A soft bump woke her. Her eyes flew open. She glanced around, but saw nothing.

She pulled the comforter to her chin and wiggled deeper into the covers.

Before her eyelids drifted closed, it came again.

Thud!

The sound, like a heavy sack hitting the floor, came from above.

She listened, heart pounding, blood surging.

Heavy footsteps paced back and forth.

*Somebody is up there.*

Her bare feet hit the cold floor as she wrestled to don her robe.

*I bet it's Winston playing tricks. Trying to scare me. I'll show him.*

Did she believe in spirits? No, but a good ghost story always got her adrenalin running.

She lit a candle and set out to find the room above her.

At the end of the hall was a narrow staircase. "This must be the way up."

The old stairs creaked a bit, so she tread lightly.

The landing opened into a hallway like the one she and the children occupied. The stairs and the passageway, covered with an undisturbed layer of dust, indicated their long disuse. *It's obvious Winston didn't come this way.*

She tried to remember where her room was in proximity to this floor. *Fourth door down, I think. On the left.*

She tip-toed until she stood in front of the corresponding door. The knob was loose, but locked. "Winston," she whispered. "Open up. You don't fool me."

Convinced he was behind the door, she rattled it harder.

No sound.

She glanced around the hallway as if something lurked in the shadows. "Maybe it's not Winston."

The candle shook in her hand sending flickering shadows along the walls.

Again, she murmured, mostly to assuage a rising panic, "I don't believe in ghosts, so fear is not an option, but an investigation is warranted."

She reached out a trembling hand. Another hard rattle of the doorknob yielded nothing.

She knocked. "Whoever's in there, I'm not frightened. Come out, at once. You might wake the children."

Dead silence.

"I mean it. Enough of this nonsense. Open the door."

Nothing.

She tried it again and to her amazement, the knob turned.

Her heart beat wildly. *Now, we'll get to the bottom of this.*

She pushed.

The door opened.

"Winston?"

She stepped into the dark room. The bright moon offered little light through the dingy lace curtains.

Nothing looked out of place. A normal parlor, covered with dust, but undisturbed.

"Winston. If this is your idea of trickery, it's not

working. You might as well show yourself."

Silence.

As her eyes adjusted, she noted several books scattered on the floor. At closer inspection, she observed one wall completely shelved with an array of reading material.

*The sky parlor. The one I saw this morning upon my arrival.*

She knelt to retrieve the displaced volumes. Most were leather-bound, valuable, soft and smooth in her hand.

*Whoever discarded these has no idea of their worth.*

Carefully, she eased them into the empty spaces on the shelf. The rest of the room was in order—dusty, worn, old and unused, but intact.

"Maybe the books simply fell off the shelf. I don't see anything else to indicate someone's been here. Everything's covered with dust. Maybe a mouse…"

A crystal carafe surrounded by five tulip-shaped sherry glasses sat in the center of a small wooden table. They wore the mantle of disuse, as well, but something odd struck her immediately. A missing stemware and the topper to the carafe.

She scanned the room as if to find the absent pieces and return them to their proper places, to no avail.

*Myrtle said a wine glass was found next to Edmund's body. The missing sherry glass, perhaps?*

Suddenly, all energy left her. She yearned for the comfort of her bed. Whether it was the night chill or lack of sleep, she'd enough adventure for one night.

*Nothing to see here. Simply a rogue mouse playing havoc.*

# Chapter FIVE

Phebe rose early, anxious to talk to Myrtle before the children awoke.

The warm kitchen smelled of bacon. Homemade biscuits, stacked on the sideboard, peaked her appetite. She almost forgot why she rushed downstairs.

"My, you're up early, Phebe. You slept soundly, then?" Myrtle's happy voice brightened the first blush of day.

"Don't expect it every morning. I didn't get as much sleep as I'd like."

Cook frowned. "And why was that? The room doesn't suit you? Or are ya homesick?"

"No, nothing like that. I heard the ghost."

The cook dropped the large metal fork. "The ghost?"

Phebe retrieved the utensil. "Yes, and I went up to check it out."

Myrtle's face turned lily-white. "Tell me you didn't."

"Why yes, I thought it was Winston playing a trick on me and was determined to catch him."

"No one's been up there in years."

"So it seems. It was very dusty."

Myrtle frowned. "Winston would never trick you. He's too prim and proper to indulge in such things."

"I didn't see him, nor did I find another way up there. Is there a hidden passageway?"

"No. No other passage." She retrieved the fork from Phebe. "Are you going to tell me what ya *did* find?"

She grabbed a biscuit and spread a large amount of butter on top. "Books. Large, leather-bound books scattered on the floor. A loud thump woke me. It happened twice. When I found the books on the floor, I figured a mouse or rat pushed them from the shelf. That would account for the noise. Someone really should rescue those old volumes. It's a shame to let them ruin."

"Books? On the floor?"

"Yes, but the strangest thing happened. The door was locked. I jiggled the knob, but it wouldn't turn. I rattled it again, and it opened."

"And you went in?"

"Of course. I wanted to catch the culprit. No one was there."

"My Lord, Phebe, don't tell the Mr. and Mrs. about this. Why, they'd fire you on the spot. No one is to go up there."

"They never told me I couldn't, only mentioned the other girls and how the sounds frightened them."

Myrtle wagged a finger. "You'll stir up a hornet's nest if you pursue this. Leave Mr. Edmund in peace."

Phebe grinned. "So, you *do* believe there's a ghost up there."

"I'm not sayin' I do, and I'm not sayin' I don't. I simply don't stick my nose where it don't belong. You'd best heed my warning."

Phebe finished her biscuit and wiped her hands on a napkin. "I found one more thing."

Myrtle rolled her eyes. "Well, you know I'm going to ask. What?"

"A missing sherry glass."

The kitchen door swung open. Winston entered.

Myrtle turned back to the bacon.

He returned the empty trays to the proper cupboard. "You're up early Phebe. Anxious to start the day with the children?"

"Just came down to say hello. Did you sleep well, Winston?"

He raised his brows. "An odd question. I always sleep well, but thank you for asking."

Myrtle handed her a heaping plate. "You best be gettin' your belly full and ready for those children. This being your first full day."

"I'll take it upstairs. Thank you." With a nod to Winston, she carried her meal up to the breakfast room.

The children took this morning's meal as a special treat with their parents in the dining room, so the time alone allowed her to contemplate the first night at the Powell's. The more she tried to make sense of what happened upstairs, the more she thought it played out like a dream.

*My over-active imagination, most likely. Myrtle's right. I need to put it out of my mind and concentrate on the children.*

In the light of day, a dream proved the more logical answer; a new place, new people, a ghost story, and the excitement of a new position.

Convinced of her own folly, she shrugged off the incident and turned to the day's curriculum.

The children bounded into the schoolroom at the stroke of eight.

Caught up in their enthusiasm, she forgot all about the adventure of the night before.

The children bent to their numbers, pencils in hand, scribbling furiously.

A sense of pride filled her. *The children respond well. Each of them wormed their way into my heart. I hope I sustain a long employment in this house.*

At mid-morning, a knock sounded on the school room door.

"Come in."

Mr. and Mrs. Powell entered.

"My wife and I came to see how you're getting along. From previous experience, the children would've wreaked havoc by now."

"Please come in. We're doing numbers." She turned to Charley. "Show your parents your work."

Charley lifted his paper with an infectious, freckled smile. "I've done ten problems this morning."

The Powell's exchanged glances.

"Why, this is incredible." Mrs. Powell walked over to Charley and inspected his paper. "And, they're correct, too."

Mr. Powell clucked his tongue. "Very nice, indeed."

Phebe sighed. "They're all doing well this morning."

Mr. Powell motioned for her to come closer.

She leaned in to catch his whispered question. "Did you sleep well last night? No disturbances?"

"The accommodations are wonderful. I slept fine. Nothing out of the ordinary."

His shoulders relaxed, and a wide smile erased the concern on his face. "Wonderful. Glad to hear it. We're most pleased at what we see. It's not our habit to interfere in the daily lessons, but since it was your first night here we felt compelled to check in. Feel free to come to us with any problems or questions that arise."

Mrs. Powell rejoined her husband. "Yes, I'm impressed. They've never taken such an interest before. You're quite gifted."

"Thank you, Mrs. Powell. The children are charming."

"We'll leave you to it." Mr. Powell stepped back to allow his wife to pass, but turned and whispered. "I didn't mention it before, but you might notice the stairway to the third floor at the end of the hall. We've closed that part of the mansion off. This house is too big for this small family. We've no use for the upper floor. It's in great disrepair, so I implore you not to wander up there. I'd hate for you to fall through some rotten board."

Phebe smiled sweetly. "I understand, Mr. Powell. There's enough to keep me busy here. I see no need to wander around. Thank you for the warning."

The door closed, and she turned her attention to Elizabet who sat primly behind her desk, hands folded on top of her work.

"Now, young lady, it's your turn. Let me see your paper."

Elizabet didn't move her hands. Instead, the amber flecks in her eyes danced with mischief. "If you don't take me upstairs with you, I'll tell Papa what you did last night."

# Chapter Six

P HEBE STEPPED BACK. "Elizabet, whatever do you mean?"

"I saw you."

"Of course, you saw me. I came into your room to bid you goodnight."

"After."

She glanced at the boys, who bent to their work and remained oblivious to the conversation. "After what, Elizabet?"

"After the noise. It happens every night. I hopped out of bed and opened my door. I saw you go upstairs."

"Oh, well, I heard something and went to check it out. There was nothing there. I believe it's simply old creaking timbers."

Elizabet shook her head. "It wasn't creaking. The sound was a thump. Like every night."

"It's none of our business. Let's get back to work."

"Not until you promise."

"Blackmail, Elizabet, really? You'll cost me my job over

a noise in a rattling old house? Is this how you got rid of the others?"

"I didn't. They were scaredy cats and left on their own. You're not afraid." Elizabet's eyes glowed. "Why, you marched right up those stairs without a blink of an eye."

"Enough, young lady. We'll get back to work or you will stand in the corner."

Elizabet smiled. "Whatever you say, Ms. Phebe. But, I *will* tell Papa."

She removed the paper from the desk and tried to focus on the numbers, but they floated before her eyes, not making any sense. *What will I do? I had no idea she saw me leave my room. If I take her with me, someone will find out. If I don't, she'll tell.*

Elizabet continued to smile at her.

*She's got me cornered.*

"My turn, Ms. Phebe, I'm finished." Benjamin waved his paper.

The interruption gave her the opportunity to extract herself from Elizabet's nefarious little web.

Elizabet didn't mention the subject again. Phebe hoped the child forgot about it, but something in her Machiavellian eyes convinced her she wouldn't let it go.

She avoided the subject of the ghost at meal time. The warning from Mr. Powell and the ultimatum from Elizabet set her on edge.

*Only one full day and I'm in jeopardy of losing my job.*

As evening approached, a dread settled over her. She promised the children one-on-one time each night. No doubt Elizabet would press her.

After she tucked the boys safely in bed, she hesitated outside of Elizabet's door.

"Come in, Ms. Phebe. No sense in standing in the hallway."

The door opened at her touch. "Can you see through doors, child?"

"No, but I can hear through walls. You told my brothers good night. I was next, that's all."

"All right. Would you like a bedtime story?"

The girl shook her head. "I want a promise."

"Elizabet, I told you. No one is allowed up there. I received fair warning from your father."

She frowned. "I don't care what Papa told you. Something's going on up there. You need to tell me what."

"Aren't you frightened?"

"No, Charley and Benjamin play tricks on me all the time. I'm used to surprises. There's a ghost. I want to see it."

"There's nothing there. No ghost, nothing."

The little girl crossed her arms. "You take me up there tonight, or I'll tell."

Phebe sighed. "Very well. But, only *if* we hear the noise."

Elizabet's frown evaporated. She threw her arms around Phebe. "I love you so much. You're already my best friend."

"I love you, too." She extracted the child's arms and tucked her in. "*If* we hear the noise, I'll come for you. Meanwhile, you need to go to sleep."

Elizabet snuggled under the covers, eyes alight with excitement.

She kissed the child, extinguished the light, and continued to her room. *I'm not about to take Elizabet up there. I'm left with one choice; go upstairs before the noises begin. If I can stop it, Elizabet will sleep through the night.*

*Last night the noise didn't start until about after midnight. I'll wait an hour, make sure she's asleep, and go upstairs. Maybe I can stop the books from falling on the floor. Or maybe I can catch the mouse.*

She didn't bother to change into her nightgown, but sat in the chair beside the bed to await her chance. It was agony watching the minutes tick by.

Finally, the clock struck the hour. She tiptoed to the door, opened it a crack to check the hall, and closed it behind her. Elizabet's door was closed, and the hall was empty.

Carefully, she scurried to the abandoned stairway.

Upstairs, she found the sky parlor and tried the knob. The door opened freely.

Inside, the quarter moon cast an eerie glow through the window. She took the rocker next to the bookshelves and sat down to wait, heart pounding, not sure if she actually wanted to see what made the thumping noise.

At first, she focused on the books, waiting for the mouse, or whatever it was, to push them to the floor. Time passed slowly and without a clock, she only guessed the time.

Occasionally, her head would nod and startle her awake.

Suddenly, something changed.

The light brightened, and a slight chill permeated the room.

Awake now, she glanced around, frightened, anticipating—.

And then, she saw a shimmering apparition materialize before her eyes.

An outline. A man.

As she blinked, a more substantial figure appeared, although still transparent. Now she noticed his manner of dress. A jacket, an ascot around his neck, but the colors were muted, nondescript. The clothes were of another time.

In the chair behind him, she watched, still as a statue, heart beating in her throat, as he moved to the book shelf. Palms perspiring, she gripped the arms of the rocker.

He didn't appear to see her.

There was a sadness on his face, but something else, as well. Determination? Anger?

He reached for a book, rifled through it as though looking for something, then moved to toss it to the floor.

Before it fell from his hand, she snatched it. "No. You mustn't make any more noise."

Startled, the apparition stopped and turned toward her. She gasped at the sight of his bright eyes. She saw them clearly. Green with amber flecks.

*Just like Elizabet's.*

# Chapter SEVEN

THE NEBULOUS FIGURE FADED.

Oddly, her initial fright dissipated, as well. Although non-threatening and somewhat vaporous, those green eyes danced with light.

*I never expected to come face-to-face with a real ghost, but here I am calm and unafraid.*

"Please don't go. I'm Phebe Whiteside. Who are you?" She reached out.

He vanished.

"Please come back. I mean no harm."

He didn't reappear.

She returned to the rocker and waited.

An hour passed. He didn't return.

"I can't sit here forever. I must teach tomorrow. I hope he's finished tossing books for tonight."

The rocker creaked as she stood and glanced around. Reluctantly, she tiptoed downstairs to her room, resigned he wouldn't come back.

She fought sleep, waiting for another thud from above, hoping quiet would prevail, and willing Elizabet to sleep through the night.

The last thought before she dozed off was of the ghost's eyes. So clear, bright, and alive. And so like Elizabet's.

---

The next morning, she waited in the classroom after breakfast. The children filed in with eagerness shining on their faces.

Today, they would practice spelling. She prepared a list of words.

Charley entered first, all wiggly and excited.

Benjamin marched in, a mature countenance etched on his young face and a book under his arm. His dark brown hair was parted and slicked down in the fashion of the day.

Elizabet wore a frown.

The children slid behind their desks and prepared for the lesson—except Elizabet.

She crossed her arms and continued to pout.

"Something wrong, dear?"

"You didn't keep your promise."

"Let me get the boys started on their spelling words. We'll talk in a minute." She passed out the words for the day's spelling bee and sent them to another corner to test each other with a warning of consequences if they didn't stay on task.

Elizabet remained sullen in her seat.

"Tell me how I broke my promise," Phebe said.

"You didn't come and get me."

"I said I would *if* I heard a noise. Well, I didn't. Did you?"

Elizabet tightened her arms and deepened her frown. "No, but you should've come anyway so we could explore."

"Now see here. We had a deal. Neither of us heard the sound last night. The noise didn't happen, so I think whatever it was left the house. Maybe we're rid of it for good."

"Well…"

"Time for lessons. No more talk of the noise or the ghost."

Phebe called the boys back to their regular desks and offered a competition. The first one to get all the words spelled correctly wins a prize.

Elizabet's pout faded. Her eyes twinkled.

*Ah! She's competitive when it concerns her brothers. A good distraction.*

The day flew by. Dinner time approached with no further reference from Elizabet about prowling upstairs.

She sent them off to their parents and decided to take a stroll around the grounds. Confined to the house since she arrived, a breath of fresh air suited her.

She chose to check out the stables but stopped to grab a few apples for the horses.

Myrtle wielded a whisk handily, attacking something in a large bowl as she entered.

"Smells heavenly." She swished a cape around her shoulders. "Do the Powell's ever ride?"

The cook frowned. "Why, I'm not sure. Mostly the horses are kept for the carriage. Going for a walk?"

"Yes, I'm desperate for a change of scenery. Think I'll start at the stables. I love animals. That's not against the rules, is it?"

"No. I'm sure it's perfectly acceptable." Myrtle dropped the spoon in the bowl and grabbed a hand towel. "Sleep well?"

"Like a baby." She opened the door and made a quick exit.

As her feet crunched along the gravel walkway, she contemplated whether it would be wise to share what transpired last night. Myrtle and Winston knew more than they cared to tell. If she made too many inquiries it might get back to her employers. However, at this point, *they* possessed the information she wanted.

*It's a dilemma, for sure.*

The stable smelled of hay and dung. The horses stamped and nickered as she walked through the center aisle.

"Anyone about?"

No one answered, so she continued, stopping at each horse and petting their velvety muzzles.

At the last stall, a young boy entered from the back door carrying two buckets. "Who are you? You shouldn't be disturbin' the horses."

Physically, she guessed his age at around twelve, but his face wore the serious scowl of someone older. Dark brown hair peeked out from under a duckbill cap and clear blue eyes regarded her with suspicion.

"I'm Phebe Whiteside, the new governess. Myrtle said it was okay to come out here."

The frown remained. "I don't know any Myrtle. You

need permission to come in here." He set the buckets down, pushed the cap to the back of his head, and straightened a strap on his coveralls.

"Why, Myrtle's the cook. What's your name?"

The boy snatched off his cap. Two pink dots appeared on his youthful face, but didn't change the scowl. "Oh, I never knew Cook had a name. Sorry. Didn't hear they hired a new teacher. Name's Jake. I'm the stable boy."

"I only arrived two days ago. First chance to come outside."

Jake replaced his cap, picked up the buckets, and headed for a stall. "I got work to do."

"I didn't mean to interrupt. You care for the horses all by yourself?"

He opened a stall door and bent to his task. "Yep, been my job for 'bout two years. I'm the man of the family now. Takin' care of my ma and my little sister."

"Why, you look so young. This is a big job for someone your age."

Water sloshed from the bucket into the trough as he poured, muffling his voice. "I'm plenty big enough. Turned twelve last month. Pa died, so I had to step up."

She reached out and steadied the stall door wondering at his resolve and strength through such adversity. "I'm so sorry. Do you live nearby?"

He pointed toward the open door. "Down that lane, 'bout a quarter of a mile, next to the family cemetery."

That news intrigued her. "Cemetery?"

He continued down each stall. "Yeah, all the generations who lived in the big house are buried there."

"Can one go there? Walk around?"

He shrugged. "Guess so. Nobody ever said ya couldn't."

"It's good to meet you, Jake. If it's all right, I'd like to come back and visit the horses. I promise I won't disturb your work."

"Fine with me. Just don't get in the way. Takes me all day to groom, feed, exercise, and all. On a tight schedule since its only me." He entered the last stall.

She wondered at the boy's abruptness but dismissed it as his desire to get his work done.

The narrow path meandered through the wooded hillside. It was a pleasant walk, one she sorely needed. More than the exercise, however, was a peaked interest in the cemetery. Might she find a clue about the ghost there?

A stone wall marked the area where the family lay their dead. An iron gate barred the opening, but swung wide at her touch. She looked around as if someone watched; an expected reaction when one enters a strange cemetery, she supposed.

The shank of evening approached as she wandered through the rows of grave markers, many more than she imagined. None of the names meant anything to her, of course, but then, only one interested her. Edmund.

Myrtle said the house was handed down through *Mrs.* Powell's family, so the Powell name wasn't among the others.

*Had she mentioned Edmund's last name?*

She couldn't remember, but so far, she didn't see any markers with the name Edmund carved into the stones. As she approached the far corner, a subtle change of air crept into the cemetery. Not cold, but more ethereal. Otherworldly. She pulled the cape tightly around her, glad for its protection.

As she came to the far corner, two granite markers graced the area, surrounded by a stone barrier. One monument stood taller than the other and was obelisk in shape. The shorter one was a weeping angel.

She crept closer.

At the edge of the stone barrier, she stopped. The temperature dropped considerably. Hoping to see Edmund's name etched across the front, she stepped over the barrier and peered closer. *Jonathan McAdams, Beloved Husband and Father.*

She turned to the other marker. *Mary McAdams, Beloved Wife and Mother.*

By the birth and death dates, Jonathan out-lived his wife by twenty years.

Mary was young.

Sadness overcame her. *Only twenty-two. I wonder how she died.*

She turned from the markers and stepped back over the barrier.

Darkness descended subtly and brought with it a damp cold. It settled in her bones like an infusion. It made her shiver. She must leave now or risk finding her way back in the blackness.

Something held her back. Was it a whisper or simply a feeling?

"By the old oak."

She felt it more than heard it and turned to look.

A lone monument, under the shade of an ancient tree, beckoned to her. It, too, was made of granite and in the same obelisk shape, only smaller. As the light disappeared she could barely make out the inscription. *Edmund McAdams, Loving Son and Brother.*

The air squeezed from her lungs. She sank to her knees. *There he is. Edmund.*

As the shock of finding him wore off, she realized the cold air pushed her down like a hand at her back. The struggle to stand caused alarm. Her face was right in front of the marker. She squinted to read the dates.

*He died only two years before Mary. He was young, too. Only twenty-four.*

As quickly as the dampness engulfed her, it relented.

She stood, looking about for the path to the gate. Her voice echoed in the lonely cemetery. "Myrtle said it might be murder."

She stole a glance at Jonathan and Mary's tombstones and gasped. A man stood over Mary's grave, weeping. A scream died in her throat when she realized it was the same apparition she saw last night.

This time, she stood still, but reached out her hand.

"Edmund."

# Chapter EIGHT

Something grabbed Phebe's elbow. She stumbled forward.

Jake caught her, a lantern in one hand. "Ms. Phebe, what are you still doing out here? It's black as pitch out."

"Jake. You gave me a fright. I guess I lost track of time. Why are you here?" She glanced back to see if the ghost was still there. It wasn't.

"I come this way home. I didn't recollect seeing you come back by the stables, so figured you might still be here. You shouldn't mess around in cemeteries at night. All sorts of things can happen."

She let him lead her down the winding path to the gate, glancing back, hoping to see Edmund, again. "It's so peaceful here. The children keep me so busy, I…"

"Well, I'm walkin' you home. There's a lot of thick woods out this way. We got prowlin' coyote and such. Wouldn't do for you to get attacked."

"It's mighty nice of you, Jake. I'm sorry to be a bother." She wanted to ask him about the ghost, but decided it wasn't proper.

He left her at the kitchen door, tipped his cap, and said goodbye.

She thanked him and went inside to find the cook pacing around the kitchen, face red, cap askew.

"Myrtle, what is wrong?"

"Oh Lordy. I thought you was snatched or something. Been peering out the window for you to come back from the stables. Where in the world did you get off to?"

She grabbed an apple off the sideboard. "No need to worry. I can take care of myself. I went for a walk. Jake told me about the path to the cemetery, so I headed there. It was farther than I thought. He found me and escorted me home."

"The cemetery? You shouldn't go there. It's not right."

"Why not? Cemeteries are peaceful places. I needed some quiet after the last two days with the children. There are a couple of stone benches along the path. I might take a book on my day off and read up there. Enjoy the birds and nature."

Myrtle stared, open-mouthed. "You want to spend your day off with dead people? Girl, you're a crazy one." She pointed a finger. "I'd stay away from that place if I were you. No good can come of hanging around there."

Phebe plopped down in a kitchen chair and took a bite from the apple. "Maybe you'd like to tell me why."

*She always gets nervous when I talk of the ghost, and now, she's uncomfortable with me going to the cemetery. If*

*I needle her enough, maybe some new information will slip out.*

Winston entered sporting his signature scowl. "The children are going to a play with their parents tonight. Our dinner will be early." He turned when he saw her. "Oh, hello, Phebe. I didn't see you there. Would you like to join us for dinner?"

"Don't mind if I do. We could enjoy a good chat." She took another bite of the juicy fruit and tossed it in the scrap box.

Myrtle finished the dinner's preparations and served up beef stew and cornbread.

They ate in silence while Myrtle continued to glance at her and frown. It was clear she didn't want her to mention the cemetery in Winston's presence.

"I say, no one has handled the children the way you do, Phebe. They like you." His frown vanished but fell short of a smile.

While she appreciated praise from one so reluctant to give it, she hoped the conversation would drift toward the history of this place. She longed to find out more about Edmund, Mary, and Jonathan, how they connected to Mrs. Powell, and discover the true mystery—Edmund's death.

"The children are a delight. Mr. and Mrs. Powell raised them well. I'm fortunate they respond as they do, given the plight of the other governesses." She glanced at them both hoping the ghost would find its way into the discussion.

Winston flinched slightly, but focused on the dish in front of him.

Myrtle remained quiet.

She persisted. "What was Mrs. Powell's maiden name? Was it McAdams?"

Winston let his spoon clatter to the bowl. "The family will return soon, I must see to my other duties." His chair scraped across the wooden floor as he hurried off.

She stared after him. "Did I say something wrong?"

Cook carried her bowl to the sideboard. "You ask too many questions. Makes Winston uncomfortable. His job is to protect and serve the family, not disclose information."

"If I'm to live here, shouldn't I gain knowledge of the family? What if the children ask about their relatives?" It was a weak argument, but the only one she could muster.

"The relatives are none of your concern. The education of their ancestry falls to their parents."

Phebe took full note of the firm look on Myrtle's face. She crossed the line. "I'm sorry. You're right, of course. Father always said I was too curious. I won't bring it up again."

"I think it's best you don't. Now, I need to get this mess cleaned up."

"Let me help. The fresh air woke me up. I couldn't sleep now if I tried. It'll feel good to dip my hands in some suds."

Myrtle's face softened. "It'd be right nice to have your company."

---

Phebe lay in her bed staring at the ceiling.

She understood, now, no information would come from either of them. It was up to her to find the answer to the mystery. Loyal to their employers, they guarded the family secrets well.

The children, settled in their beds, should be asleep by now. Relieved Elizabet didn't bring up the ghost, she tucked her in and left swiftly.

Moonlight filtered through the curtains. She knew the thumping would start soon if she didn't stop it. Her arm tangled in the heavy robe as she struggled to pull it on.

Upstairs, she stood in front of the parlor door, anxious, but excited. *Will he appear?*

She didn't bother to knock, but pushed the door open.

He was there, staring at her, the amber flecks in those green eyes glowing like fire.

This time he didn't turn away.

# Chapter NINE

THE AIR VIBRATED AS PHEBE AND THE GHOST regarded each other. Goosebumps sprang to her arms as a chill engulfed the room.

A glow radiated from his body and bathed the room in a vaporous light.

She whispered, "Please don't go, Edmund."

His eyes remained vibrant, but he didn't disappear. The sight of him standing in the light was beautiful. More than the eyes, now, she saw the shock of dark hair, the strong jaw and rugged look of him.

Encouraged, she pressed more. "I'm Phebe Whiteside. We've seen each other before. May I come in?"

"You were in the cemetery tonight." Edmund's voice rolled in a low timber, like velvety warm chocolate, smooth and full.

"Yes, I was searching for you."

He looked away. The light dimmed, the hum diminished.

Afraid he might dissolve again, she stepped into the room and gathered the books off the floor. "Were you reading?"

"Reading? No." He faded a bit, but his eyes glowed brighter, the amber flecks shooting infinitesimal shards of light right at her. "Why are you here? What do you want?"

"I'm the new governess." She held the intense gaze, fighting to maintain her composure. The glowing orbs cut into her soul, pulled her in as if they might swallow her up. Despite the ferocity of his scrutiny, she smiled and spoke softly, "You make quite a lot of noise at night. I came to investigate the sound."

"I'm searching for the diary."

When he spoke, his form solidified, the colors of his clothes came alive, the forest green corduroy waistcoat adorned his upper body, the ascot was a deep scarlet.

"Diary? Your diary?"

"No, Mary's."

"Jonathan's wife?"

He faded instantly.

"Please, come back, Edmund."

His form strengthened until he appeared solid again, eyes brighter, the shooting particles of amber piercing her soul. "Never speak his name, again. Mary is mine."

"I'm sorry. I wasn't aware. Perhaps you'd like to tell me why you're searching for the diary. I can help you look." She went to the rocker, heart pounding, and sat down.

The light surrounding him dissipated until he appeared like any other flesh and blood man. "I must find it. We can't be together until I do."

A winged-back chair sat adjacent to the rocker. She pointed to it. "Please, sit down and talk. I'm a friend. I want to help you."

He studied her, the conflict on his face evident by a slight frown. The glow in his eyes lost the intense brightness, but he did as she asked.

Phebe leaned back in the rocking chair trying to show a calmness she didn't feel. "Mary is the woman you love?"

"Yes." The force in his voice rattled the sherry glasses on the mirrored tray.

She wanted to ask questions but understood the fragile nature of this new friendship. *Friendship with a ghost? Is that possible?*

He rose and returned to the bookcase. "I must look. I don't have much time."

"You promised to tell me about her."

He gazed at the books until one flew from the shelf.

She caught it in mid-air. "You mustn't make so much noise, Edmund."

His lips parted, as if to speak, one brow lifted in surprise.

"I'm Phebe. Have you forgotten so soon?"

"Phebe…"

"Yes, your friend."

"I need to find the diary."

"You told me. I want to help, but you must explain this to me. I can't help you if you don't tell me your story."

"It's Mary. I have to help her, so we can be together."

At this point, she couldn't surmise if Edmund realized he was dead or not. If she said the wrong thing, he might disappear forever.

He sat down and bowed his head. "If I don't find the diary, I can't release her from the hell she endures."

"Edmund, do you; I mean…you understand that you are, well…"

His eyes flashed bright as he looked up. "Dead? We all are. Mary, me, and—*him*."

"Why is it so important for you to find this diary, if you are all…"

"Because of the lies. Everything was a lie. He stole Mary from me. I can't let him get away with it. Mary can't rest. She wants *me*. We want to be together."

"I don't understand. She is buried beside her husband. Does that mean she married your brother?"

The room exploded with light and vibration. Books flew off the shelves in a violent barrage. Edmund stood in the middle of the floor, hands outstretched, writhing in agony, his face contorted with rage.

"Stop! You must stop. You'll wake the whole house with this racket." She hastily gathered books from the floor, as if it would remove the noise peppering the ceiling of the second floor.

He stood still.

Books stopped flying.

His eyes returned to a soft glow while he lowered his arms.

Out of breath, she stood holding several books. "What happened? Why in the world are you so angry?"

Remorse replaced the rage on his face. "I'm sorry. I've not yet learned to control emotion in this realm."

Annoyed, she shoved the books back on the shelves, one by one. "Well, you've had plenty of time to practice. I should think you would after all these years."

After she replaced the last book, she turned to him. "Now, sit down and tell me what made you so angry."

His face took the form of a contrite child, but he reclaimed the chair.

*He's a lost soul. Fighting some kind of demon, something not settled before his death. My heart goes out to him.*

His eyes filled with wonder as he studied her. "I've never seen anyone before. You are the first one. And, how is it you can see me?"

"I don't know. I'm certainly not one who goes around seeing ghosts. The fact remains, we have crossed paths for some reason. Maybe I'm the one who can help you, but you must tell me everything. Start at the beginning, maybe we can sort this out."

He stared at her as if his eyes could drill a hole right through her, the amber flecks pulsating, threatening. "I was murdered."

# Chapter TEN

The night passed quickly as Edmund revealed his story.

She listened, afraid to stop or interrupt him about things she didn't understand.

"I met Mary at a church social." His face relaxed as he said her name. The hard line of his jaw softened. "She was the most beautiful girl I'd ever seen. We fell into a comfortable kinship, immediately. Her father, a prominent parson in town, gave his permission for us to see one another. We fell in love."

She nodded. "Go on."

"As time went on, I asked for her hand in marriage. The parson agreed, but insisted on a long engagement, parties, the proper announcements, and such. A year."

He glanced up, eyes soulful and pleading. "One whole year."

She remained silent, waiting.

"As the wedding day approached, Mary came to me,

wanted to tell me something, but *he* interrupted."

Phebe spoke softly. "He?"

His eyes resumed a fierce glow. "My younger brother."

Suddenly, she understood. "Jonathan."

The hum grew loud, again, the room vibrated, and books dropped off the shelves.

"Don't say his name!"

"Please, Edmund, stop. I'm sorry. I won't say it again. You need to stay calm."

"I'm sorry. I can't control it."

"Close your eyes, think of Mary and all the happy times you enjoyed together.

He did as she asked. The hum weakened, the vibration stopped, as did the gravity defying books.

"Good. So, we've learned something, Edmund. When these things overwhelm you, think of Mary. You can control this, you simply must focus."

He opened his eyes. "Thank you. You're right. The anger subsides if I train my thoughts on her."

"Can you go on? What did Mary want to tell you?"

His form shimmered, became vaporous, like a fine mist. "I must go. I told you I didn't have much time."

"No, please, I need more information. Please stay."

"It's not up to me. I'm only allowed a short time to discover the truth. I'm sorry."

"Will you come back tomorrow?"

As he dissolved completely, she barely caught his whisper, "I'll try."

And then, he was gone.

The books strewn across the floor remained the only

clues he was there at all. She picked them up and placed them back on the shelf.

The sky lightened through the window.

"I've been up here all night. How will I ever get through the day?"

She hurried downstairs to her room. The clock chimed five bells. "I must be up by six o'clock. I've no time to sleep. I'll just lay on the bed, close my eyes, and pray the racket Edmund made didn't wake the others."

Sleep didn't come. Instead, she stared at the ceiling and replayed the image of Edmund's tortured ghost: his eyes, the anger, the sadness. So many questions popped into her head. Why was he there? Why could she see him? Was it her imagination? Was he even there, at all?

The clock announced six a.m. She could take another hour and try to sleep. Class time was eight o'clock. It wouldn't do to change her routine now, however. Each morning, she bounded into the kitchen promptly at seven. Myrtle and Winston might question her absence. She wasn't prepared to share the events of last night. Not yet.

She sat up, changed her clothes, took extra care with her morning ablutions, and brushed her long hair. She studied herself in the mirror. *It won't do to look disheveled. My eyes are like sandpaper. I hope my lack of sleep isn't obvious.*

The aroma of pancakes triggered hunger.

"Mornin' Phebe," Myrtle said.

The normal cheer usually displayed became forced. "Good morning."

Myrtle moved the large mixing bowl to one side, squinting at her. "What's wrong with *you* this morning? You look as if you didn't sleep a wink."

"Nothing's wrong. I read far into the night. Didn't get my proper winks. I'll pay for it today, but it is such a great tale." She poured a cup of coffee and sat down.

"And what are ya readin'?"

"Moby Dick. My parents gave it to me for my birthday. I'm almost finished. Have you read it?"

A derisive snort emanated from Myrtle's rather large nose. "You won't find me reading any books. I ain't got time for such idle pastimes."

"Reading is educational. Educating the children is why I'm here, remember? You really should pick up a book, occasionally."

Cook snorted again.

Phebe paused. "I meant to ask you…I'm almost finished with it. Do you think Mrs. Powell would mind if I looked for another in the library? They do have a library, don't they?"

"Yes, of course. It's kept locked, but I don't see as they'd mind. You should ask this morning, however. They're leaving with the children after lessons."

"Where are they going? Am I to go along?"

"Well, I can't say for sure, you only arrived a few days ago. It's their tradition for the family to visit Mr. Powell's Aunt Martha, once a month. This is the weekend. I doubt they expect you to go."

In between bites, she tried to ask more questions, but the rich, buttery flavor of the pancakes only accentuated her ravenous hunger.

"I've never seen you eat so, Phebe. Does reading make

you that hungry?"

She laughed, almost spewing a mouthful. "I can't say it's reading that makes me hungry. Maybe the lack of sleep."

"Well, don't nod off in the middle of your lessons."

A knock on the door interrupted the light-hearted banter.

Myrtle greeted the young stable boy. "Why Jake, what brings you to the house so early?"

He snatched the cap from his head. "Mr. Powell asked me to ready the horses. I left the house so quick this morning I plumb forgot the carrots for Artemis. He gets a bit cranky if he doesn't get them. I wonder if you have some to spare."

"Come on in, I'm sure I can scare up a few."

"Oh no, I can't come in. I've mud on my boots."

Phebe was pleased to see her friend. "Good morning, Jake."

"Morning, a pleasant day to ya."

He grabbed the carrots. "Much obliged."

"I might have some time on my hands this afternoon. I'd like to visit the stables again, with your permission." She pushed the chair back and followed him.

"Anytime, Ms. Phebe. I really must go. Artemis won't be easy to handle without his treat."

She watched him walk toward the barn.

"Shut the door, girl. You're lettin' the flies in."

"Sorry. He's such a polite young man. Carries a lot of work on his shoulders. He told me his pa used to work the stables until he died. I would think they'd replace him with a grown man, not a young boy."

"There ya go. Asking more questions. The runnin' of the stables is a family affair. Jake's family has carried on the tradition since the family arrived here. Now, put your curious nose back where it belongs. You better get to the classroom."

The statement was issued with more force than Phebe expected, adding another layer of inquisitiveness to the mix.

She folded all the bits and pieces of this curious household away and tucked them into her mental 'to do' list. *I'll deal with this later.*

As she turned to go, Winston entered, the ever-present scowl in place.

"The Powell's wish to see you in the study. Now."

## Chapter ELEVEN

P HEBE OPENED THE STUDY DOOR, HANDS SHAKING. Had her employers heard the noise last night? Were they aware she went up to the third floor?

The couple sat together much like they did when she first met them. Mr. Powell behind the polished desk, Mrs. Powell on the chaise.

Mr. Powell stood, but didn't extend his hand. "Good morning, Phebe."

She couldn't read his face, and her heart beat thudded in her chest. She curtsied. "Good morning, sir. Good morning, ma'am."

Mr. Powell nodded. "I'm not sure we mentioned our monthly excursions to my Aunt Martha's. It's a half day's carriage ride. We take the children to visit her. She loves them so."

"Myrtle mentioned something."

He sat down again. "Yes, well, after lessons we'll be on our way. No need for you to make the trip as there won't be any time for schooling. Is there anything you need while we're gone? I trust you may enjoy a couple of days off after this first few days with the children."

"I'll miss them, of course. I look forward to the chance to catch up on my reading, however. Is it possible for me to make use of your library? I'm almost finished with the book I brought with me.

Mr. Powell looked at his wife. "I don't see any reason why you can't make use of our collection. I'll have Winston give you a key. We keep it locked due to the number of precious editions."

"Thank you so much. I'll take great care."

"Good, I'm sure the children await their lessons. We'll see you when we return."

She curtsied again and turned to leave, relieved no mention of the previous night's melee was made.

---

The children resorted to fidgeting during class time. She chalked it up to excitement of the up-coming trip and allowed them a little slack.

Elizabet's face beamed when the lessons concluded.

"You're excited to see your great-aunt this weekend, Elizabet?"

"Oh yes, she's my favorite. Her house is big, with a huge porch that goes all around the house. I love to play there. She has two dogs. I especially like fishing because I always catch the most." Her enthusiasm rushed out of her.

She smiled. "It all sounds wonderful. Have a good time."

"You aren't coming with us?"

"Not this time, dear. I've lessons to prepare for next week."

Elizabet frowned, slightly, but the smile returned in an instant.

Phebe hugged each of them as they left.

From an upstairs window, she watched the carriage pull away with Mr. Powell at the reins.

Now, she had the opportunity to look around, and maybe, find clues to Edmund's dilemma. *He's looking for a diary. Maybe he's looking in the wrong place.*

Footsteps sounded on the stairway.

Winston's white head popped into view. "Mrs. Powell asked me to give you the key to the library. She said you liked to read." He held out his hand.

She took it. "Yes, thank you. I've almost finished Moby Dick. I'll have two long days without anything to pass the time. They were gracious to allow me permission."

"See that you're careful. Mrs. Powell has worked extensively to preserve the collection they've gathered over the years."

"Of course, Winston. I love books as much as they do."

He nodded and left her by the window.

Fatigue suddenly overwhelmed her. She decided to skip lunch and treat herself to a nap. She sighed as the soft bed embraced her and fell asleep immediately.

When she woke, the sun was down, light in the room dimmed.

*How long did I sleep?* The clock showed five-thirty-five.

She hurried downstairs.

A note pinned on the cupboard caught her attention in the empty kitchen.

*Winston and I go home to our families on this weekend. Since you didn't come down for lunch I didn't have a chance to tell you. We'll be back Sunday eve. Hope you rest well. There's plenty of food in the ice box. M.*

The light in the window faded, as did her resolve.

*I'm completely alone.*

She scurried around to light a large candle on the table, fumbling for the match box by the stove. When light illuminated the room, her courage returned.

*I have no idea how to use the gas lights in this house. I must rely on the candles.*

At the table, she watched the flame dance, casting shadows across the walls.

"Silly me, I shouldn't have fallen asleep. I'm starved. First thing is to get something to eat."

A roast beef sandwich on sourdough bread satisfied her immediate hunger. She noted there was plenty to last for two days. "Bless you, Myrtle."

She picked up the candle and headed into the great hall. The library door across from the study beckoned to her, but the key was upstairs.

The house was eerily quiet, despite the creaking timbers and the wind blowing outside. The larger candles were kept in the bottom kitchen drawer. She retrieved several and made her way upstairs.

The key fit perfectly in the small pocket of her dress. A quick pat of the pocket and armed with the biggest candle, she set off.

Heavy green drapery gave the library an eerie feel. Not one ray of moonlight peeked through. The candle provided just enough light to see the titles as she skimmed across the rows.

*So many wonderful literary works here. I'm in heaven.*

Each book she pulled from the shelves made her heart flutter as she thumbed through pages she only dreamt about reading. Sometimes, she sat down and read a few passages of a particular volume. Excited to find even more treasures, however, she lay each book on the desk for future exploration.

The flickering light cast shadows on the walls, but she hardly noticed, lost in the joy of being surrounded with so many great works. She wasn't sure how much time passed, hours maybe, until the wind rattled the windows and caught her attention. A storm was blowing in. Suddenly, she remembered.

*Edmund!*

# Chapter TWELVE

THE STORM ADVANCED QUICKLY, MAGNIFYING EVERY sound, every shadow, as Phebe hurried to stop Edmund's inevitable onslaught. The candle threatened to extinguish in her haste. She cupped one hand around the bobbing flame and continued.

On the second floor, thumping broke the silence.

*He's here!*

Her pace quickened until she stopped in front of the sky-parlor door, gasping for air. She pushed it open.

"Edmund. Stop."

He stared at her, a book in each hand, brows knit. "You?"

"Yes, I'm late, but I'm here."

He stumbled over her name. "Phe…be? Ms. Phebe. I thought you weren't coming."

"I said I would."

He looked at the books on the floor. "I can't find it. I must find the diary." His eyes glowed, his body was slightly transparent, but the sadness on his face expressed utter pain.

"I know, Edmund. We must figure this out. I'm here to help you."

"But, how? I look every night, but never find it."

"Maybe you're looking in the wrong place. Why do you always look here, in this room?"

His brow furled, he squinted, as if seeking an answer. "I don't know. I've tried to leave, but I can't. The knob won't turn, I can't grasp it. I'm trapped here every night."

"But, I've seen you in the cemetery. I know you can appear in other places."

"It's Mary. I can go see Mary's grave."

"Any other graves?"

"No, only hers."

"None of this makes sense, Edmund, but I'm going to try. You are stuck in the room where you died."

"Where I was murdered."

"Yes, murdered. You visit Mary at her grave. You are stuck in a pattern of some kind. Maybe I'm supposed to disrupt it."

"How?"

"I don't know. I've never seen a ghost before, only heard stories. My brothers used to scare me with frightening tales of spirits lurking in the woods, but to no avail. My personality isn't bent toward things of this nature. I'm a no-nonsense type of person. Practical. Logical. So, if I can see you, something is afoot. A mystery needs to be solved. It's the only explanation." She put the books back on the shelf and took her seat in the rocking chair.

Edmund followed suit, settling in the winged-back

chair. "I've never seen anyone in all this time, only this room and Mary's grave. I do play the scene, over and over, in my mind, however."

"The scene?" She leaned forward.

"Yes, the night he poisoned the sherry."

"So, it was poison. And Jonathan did it?"

The room shook, Edmund's eyes took on the familiar fierce glow, the amber shards sent shocks of light around the parlor. "It had to be him."

Phebe tried to calm him. "Mary, think of Mary. She wants you to be in control while we figure this out."

Slowly, his eyes returned to their normal color, the amber darts retreating into a sea of green. The room ceased to vibrate. He whispered, "Mary."

After he took on a solid form, she resumed, "Did you see him put the poison in the glass? Was he in the room when you drank it?"

He frowned. "I didn't actually see him pour it. We talked of my wedding. Mary's and mine. I shared our happiness, our hope for the future, talked of her beauty. He didn't reply, just observed me with the dark hooded look he gets when he's up to no good. Eyes half closed like he's bored to death. I don't know why I told him. He was always jealous of me because I was older."

"So, he offered you a drink and you took it."

"Not exactly, I poured the sherry. But, he was there."

She scratched her head. "Why does Mary keep telling you to find the diary?"

He blinked several times. "She says the answer is in there."

"Answer? Then, she knows it was your brother who murdered you?"

"I don't know. She always persists I find the diary, that it tells of something I should know."

"Are you able to see Mary, talk with her?"

The amber light in his eyes dimmed. "No, I don't see her. I hear her voice. It whispers to me."

"So, she's unable to cross over to you, I suppose. Stuck in time, perhaps?" She walked to the door. "We don't have much time. The family will return Sunday evening. We only have two days to figure this out. Come. Let's try something."

He followed her. "Try what? What can we do?"

"Try to step over the threshold. The door is open now, so no problem with the doorknob."

The floor held his attention, eyes fixed on the doorstop. He looked up briefly, then lifted his foot.

"That's it, go ahead and cross over."

A slight buzzing filled the room. His foot stopped just short of the open door.

"I can't. Something is pushing me back."

As soon as he lowered his foot, the buzzing stopped.

Phebe stepped over the threshold. "Nothing stops me. It has to be from the other realm." She re-entered the room. "So, we'll have to try something else. Where is Mary's bedroom?"

"To the right, two doors down."

"I'll be right back. Please don't throw any more books on the floor while I'm gone." She started to leave.

"Wait." He took her hand.

To her surprise, the connection was instant, his hand

was warm and strong. She trembled.

"Why are you doing this, Phebe? I'm nothing to you. Why would you take a chance for me?"

Their eyes locked. The green brightened when he looked at her, the amber flecks danced. His intense scrutiny burrowed into her soul.

Breathless, she whispered. "It seems I am the one chosen to solve this mystery, and…because you deserve to have answers." Carefully, she extracted her hand and tried to slow her heartbeat, looking past him to the winged-back chair. "Wait over there. I won't be long."

The darkened hallway made her pause and grab the candle from the table. A lightning bolt lit up the sky and thunder rattled the windows. The storm didn't appear to phase Edmund as she glanced back at him. He sat straight in the chair, hands on his knees, looking at the bookshelves.

*Why am I doing this? He's a ghost.*

The touch of his hand stirred emotion in her. She never had a beau. Her life was complete caring for children. But somehow, his touch awakened an emptiness she long buried.

*Too late for me, but at least, I can help Edmund and Mary reunite in the afterlife. I must find that diary, so he can go to Mary.* She hurried forward, looking right and left. *Do other ghosts inhabit this house? Are there more secrets hidden up here?*

The door to Mary's room squeaked when she pushed. She held the candle forward to light the room, peeked her head inside, and let her eyes adjust.

A large canopy bed draped with rose cloth at the

corners caught her eye immediately. A chaise lounge sat on the left wall, a rocking chair on the right, both covered in a beautiful rose pattern. Beside the bed was a lovely, white bassinet.

*A baby. No one mentioned a baby. The cemetery showed Mary and Jonathan married after Edmund's death. They must have a child together.*

She whispered to the empty room. "How very odd. Everything in the *parlor* is covered with dust. There isn't any in here. Someone is taking care of this room. But who?"

She glanced to the left. A large bookcase stood in the corner. "Ah, here we are. I bet the diary is here."

Flashes of lightning added some illumination. She held the candle in one hand and ran her index finger over the books, one by one, hoping to discover the diary. Row by row, she continued, her left-hand fighting fatigue from the weight of the large candle. The bottom row was impossible to see. She placed the candle on the floor and knelt on the cold wood floor. Still no sign of a diary.

She retrieved the light, knees protesting as she stood. "Now what?"

A slow scan of the room revealed a nightstand by the bed. The small drawer opened at her touch. She glanced inside. "Notepads, writing utensils, a scented sachet…"

Shadows danced across the walls as she moved from the drawer to the center of the room. "If I were Mary where would I hide my diary?"

She looked at the bed, the bassinet, the book shelves. "Under the mattress, maybe."

Nothing.

Then, she spied a small travel trunk in a corner beside the chaise.

The latch wasn't locked, and the lid lifted easily. On top lay neatly folded dresses, under those, lace undergarments. Shoe boxes rested on one side. Baby things on the other.

"Someone packed for a trip. Could the diary be…" She slid her hand deeper under the clothes and wiggled around until her fingers hit a solid object. A book.

She pulled it out, opened it towards the middle, and read, *Dear Diary. Jonathan confessed to me today.*

# Chapter
## THIRTEEN

A LIGHTNING BOLT FLASHED AND BATHED THE leather cover of a well-used journal in a bright light. An ominous clap of thunder followed as the light faded.

Phebe said aloud, "I found it."

She flipped it open, but immediately snapped it shut. The words she read hung in the air. *Dear Diary. I met the most wonderful man today. His name is Edmund.*

"This is wrong. These are Mary's innermost thoughts." As she struggled with the pang of conscience, she rationalized. "The answers are here, but how can I intrude in this dead woman's past? Her confessions are not meant for other's eyes. I can't do it."

The book lay lightly in her hand. The journal wasn't fancy, simply plain and ordinary.

A shadow crossed the window.

She shivered. *A dark cloud. The storm must be over.*

The wind ceased, thunder rolled in the distance, but

outside, the rain stopped and calm replaced the rampage.

"Edmund must see this. He'll be so pleased I found it. It's his to read, not mine."

She closed Mary's door and hurried to the sky-parlor.

The door hung half open, but the room was dark even with the candle. There was no sign of her ghostly friend.

"Edmund?" she whispered.

No answer.

"He's gone." She studied diary. "Will he come back? What am I to do with this?"

She waited in the doorway, hoping for his return, but finally returned to the rocker. "I'll wait. Maybe the storm scared him off."

An hour passed, still no sign of him. The temptation to open the journal and read more almost took over in the eerie silence, but she held firm.

"Edmund must read it first."

Another half hour passed.

"He's not coming back tonight."

Reluctant to leave, she stood and walked slowly to the door with one more hopeful glance behind her.

---

In her room, she put the book on the nightstand and stared at it. "What if finding the diary sent Edmund back to the unknown? What if he never comes back? Do I dig deeper or do I put this back and forget it exists?" She paced, shaking her head, trying to reason. "He appears because Mary told him to find the diary. If I put it back, he might reappear.

Oh, what shall I do?"

A decision must be made before the family's return. If finding the diary freed Edmund from the nightly agony he'd suffered since his murder, then maybe the purpose was fulfilled. But, to what end?

"This isn't my business. This family has secrets, but it's not up to me to reveal them."

Instead of sleep, she tossed and turned, wrestling with the heavy weight on her shoulders. "Myrtle did warn me to mind my own business."

The next morning, it was hard to open her eyes against the sun streaming through the window. "But, I must start the day. I'll worry about the journal tonight."

Downstairs, a knock interrupted the meager breakfast she managed to scare up. After a last swig of milk, she opened the door to Jake.

"Good morning, Ms. Phebe. I watched the family leave yesterday and didn't see you with them. Cook and Winston always go home on these weekends, so I figured you must be all alone. Thought I'd stop by and see how you are faring in this old house, all alone."

"Hello, Jake. You're certainly a sight for sore eyes. My first night alone was a bit intimidating, but I got through it. Come in. I was finishing breakfast."

For the first time, he smiled at her, restoring a more childlike countenance, casting away the more serious man-of-the-family look.

"Don't mind if I do. I could use a cup of milk."

"Good."

She poured as he perched on a stool.

He took a big gulp. "Anything you need help with? I'm done with my chores. I'll be back this afternoon to feed the horses again."

"I *could* use some help with the gas lights. I fumbled through the night with candles."

He laughed. "With the storm and all? You're one brave lady."

"I don't know about that, but I survived."

He slid off the stool. "Well, let's get to it. Maybe tonight won't be so scary."

After the lesson, Jake bid her goodbye. "I can come back tonight if you like."

She hesitated. *It would be nice to have company, but what if Edmund comes back?*

"Thanks so much, Jake, but I'll be fine. If I can get through a night with a storm using only candles, I can make it tonight. You're needed at home."

"Well, if you change your mind, leave a note in the barn by the first stall. I'll come running." He opened the door and was gone.

His sturdy walk toward the barn revealed his sense of purpose. *He certainly takes his responsibilities seriously. I wish he could stay for a while.*

When he disappeared into the barn, she closed the door. "I have next week's lessons to prepare. I better get to it."

The classroom kept her mind from the events of the previous night. She managed to complete a whole week of lesson plans. At lunch time, she wandered into the kitchen and satisfied her growling stomach with another of Myrtle's sandwiches.

"Wonder if Jake has returned?"

She wandered outside and ducked inside the barn. "Jake? Are you in here?"

When there was no answer, she passed the stalls and spoke to each horse. The last few stalls were empty, the horses in service to the family.

The day smelled fresh after the torrential rain and she decided to take a walk. Curiosity got the better of her. She headed to the cemetery. "If I can't read the diary, I *can* look at the public headstones."

The path showed signs of the storm with leaves and debris, but she picked her way through and entered the gate.

When she reached the back corner, she quickly found Edmund's resting place.

"Hello, Edmund. Where did you go last night? I have news for you. I found the diary and started to read it, but decided you should be the first. Please come visit tonight. I want to show you."

She didn't expect any response, it was broad daylight. He'd never appeared during the day. As she turned to leave, she stopped in front of Mary's grave. "What do you know, Mary? What is your secret? Will its reveal help Edmund rest in peace?"

"What are you doing back here, Ms. Phebe?"

She whirled at the sound of Jake's voice. "Do you always sneak up on people?"

"Sorry, I was headed back to the barn, when I saw you here. Your red headscarf stands out, ya know." He grinned, showing deep dimples.

She reached up and adjusted the scarf. "I didn't think

anyone would object to my taking a walk. It's peaceful here."

"You've come to this spot before. Do you know somebody buried here?"

"Why no, just meandered around, found myself in this corner."

"Naw, don't buy it. You were gawkin' pretty hard at Mrs. McAdams tombstone. You curious 'bout her?"

She cocked her head. "Now, what would I be curious about?"

"How she died. What happened to the baby."

"Baby? So, you know about the baby?"

He took her elbow and pulled her toward the gate. "Rumors abound in these parts."

She tried to steady her heartbeat. "What information would one glean from those rumors?"

"I've got too much to do this afternoon. Not enough time to gossip about the towns secrets. You'll just have to wonder." He laughed as he pulled her along.

They parted at the barn.

One more time, she entered the empty house with no more information than before.

A large yawn escaped. "The fresh air made me sleepy. I may have a long night ahead of me. A nap is in order."

She fell asleep with Edmund's handsome face dancing in her head. *I hope he returns. I'll miss him if he doesn't.*

## Chapter FOURTEEN

Phebe's resilient personality and strong resolve almost failed her as a reign of heavy thumping sounded overhead. She usually faced things head on, wide-eyed and with a bent toward logic. This time, however, the noise was different, more like boots tromping back and forth, and it sent a chill right through her.

"What in the world?"

Startled from sleep, it took a second to adjust to her surroundings. She fixed her gaze on the ceiling. *He's back. Edmund is back.*

Hurriedly, she patted her hair in place, smoothed her dress, and ran out the door. "Oh, I forgot the journal." She rushed back to retrieve it, glanced at the clock beside the bed, and scampered back to the stairs.

"It's midnight. He sounds very upset."

At the parlor door, she waited, almost losing her nerve.

She pushed the door open. He stood before her, eyes blazing.

"Edmund!"

"It's past midnight, I've been waiting for you to come." His voice boomed so loudly it rattled the glassware on the table.

She drew herself to full height and issued a reprimand. "You may recall I was up half the night searching for the diary. And *you* were nowhere to be found when I returned. I've had little sleep and am in a foul mood. I'd tread lightly if I were you."

Surprised at the force of her own words, she stood her ground, chin uplifted in defiance, but heart pounding at the reality of what she'd done. *I just scolded a ghost.*

Edmund's eyes lost their fire, his shoulders dropped like a recalcitrant child. "I'm sorry. When you didn't come back, I thought you deserted me."

"Well, I didn't leave you. I came back. *You* left me."

He whispered, "I had no choice. My time was up."

After her heartbeat resumed its normal rhythm, she indicated the chairs. "I found something. I want you to see it."

"You found the diary?"

"Yes, sit down. I opened it only long enough to verify it was Mary's. I didn't read further. It was in a traveling trunk in the corner of her room."

He sat down, trembling. "A traveling trunk?"

"Yes, it appears she was about to take a trip. Her clothes were inside, along with baby things—and this." She stretched out her hand.

Edmund took the book and studied it, but didn't open it. "Baby things?"

She watched him try to process the news about a baby, watched the confusion pinch his face. It dawned on her—*he doesn't know.*

Gently, she asked him, "Did you know Jonathan married Mary after your death, er, murder?"

The room rattled again with Edmund's anger. "No! Not my Mary."

"It's true, Edmund. The proof is in the cemetery. I'm surprised you haven't noticed it. They're graves are side-by-side. Mr. and Mrs. Jonathan McAdams."

This time, the explosion reached a deafening level as books flew, glasses rattled, doors slammed, and Edmund became a whirl of light and smoke.

She shouted above the fray, "Edmund, stop. You must stop it now. Mary wanted you to know. You have to read the diary."

Slowly, the room stopped vibrating, his ghost-like appearance became clearer until he was a solid entity once more.

"Why would she marry *him*? He didn't love her. Why? Please tell me why."

"She left this for you. I'm sure she explains it all in here."

He took the book but didn't open it.

"Are you going to read it or simply stare at it? You'll get your answers now."

He looked at her, his countenance soft, vulnerable, like a small boy who lost his way. "Yes, answers."

She studied his face, noted the strong jaw line, the hint of a dimple, the Romanesque nose, and those eyes. Green with flecks of amber. *He certainly is a handsome man.*

He opened the book and read.

He whispered low, "She was leaving him."

"Why?"

Edmund dropped the diary on the floor. "He confessed to her."

She picked it up. "Confessed what? To murdering you?"

"No, something more sinister."

"Well, are you going tell me or do I have to read it for myself?"

Like a candle snuffed out, Edmund disappeared.

She blinked in disbelief, book in hand. "Edmund?"

The room turned cold, as if life had left it.

"Please don't go. Don't leave."

No amount of pleading brought him back. He was gone, and she feared would never return.

Finally, she looked at the diary left in the chair. *This is where I will find the answer he so desperately sought.*

Reluctantly, she headed downstairs to her room, the diary clutched tight. She laid it on the nightstand, sat on the side of the bed, and stared at it.

"The family will come home tomorrow. I don't know what to do with this book. It won't do to show anyone, and I can't reveal what I've done."

The gaslights flickered.

In the silence, she heard a frantic knocking coming from downstairs.

"Someone at the door, at this hour? But, who would come here in the middle of the night?"

Undecided, she waited. "Maybe they'll go away. A lost traveler perhaps? They mustn't know I'm alone."

A muffled voice called for her to open the door.

Once more, the rapping resumed on the kitchen door, a familiar voice persisting.

She rushed down the stairs to the kitchen, unlatched the lock, turned the doorknob, and pulled it open.

## Chapter Fifteen

Phebe gasped at the sight of Jake standing in the doorway. "Whatever are you doing out this time of night?"

His round eyes and knit brows reflected a concerned look, replacing his normal matter-of-fact countenance. "I was outside trying to see why Zeke was barking so fiercely. There was a… uh…light."

She took his arm and pulled him inside, ready to close the door against the darkness.

Zeke stood beside the door, his dark, shaggy coat damp, eyes wary. Both ears stood at attention.

The boy stood in the middle of the kitchen and pointed to the dog. "Can Zeke come in? I don't want to leave him outside alone."

She stepped aside, and the dog trotted inside.

"I don't understand. What kind of light?"

"A bright, flashing light."

After guiding him to a stool, she persisted. "Where?"

He paused. "In the cemetery."

"Are you sure it wasn't lightning?"

He shook his head and pointed to the window. "There's no storm tonight. Wasn't lightning. It stayed in one place—the place you always go."

The milk gurgled heavily as she poured it from the bottle. She handed him the glass. "Here, drink this."

Her mind raced to make sense of what he said. *Light in the cemetery, by Edmund's grave.*

Jake gulped the milk, plunked the glass on the table, and wiped his mouth with the back of his hand. "That's not all." He glanced at the milk bottle and back at his glass, but didn't continue.

"Well, are you going to tell me?"

"I also saw a light in the upstairs window of *this* house seconds before."

This time, she sat down.

Both remained silent, simply staring at one another.

Zeke curled up at her feet as if he'd known her forever.

Still unable to process what Jake said, she gazed at the dog instead. "What breed is he?"

"Zeke? Don't know. Mutt, I'd say. Found him along the road one day and brought him home."

"Well, he's a fine dog. You're lucky to have him."

"You know somethin' about the light. I see it on your face." He reached down and scratched Zeke's ears, his voice softer. "Wanna tell me what's going on?"

She hesitated. "If I tell you, do you promise not to breathe a word of this to anyone?"

He nodded. "I promise."

"Cross your heart?"

He made the sign across his chest. "Cross my heart."

She stood and paced the kitchen, the decision to tell him weighed heavy, but simply to have someone to talk to about the whole thing would relieve her mind.

Jake watched her, twisting around as she came behind him.

"All right. I'll tell you. It's the ghost."

He didn't speak, only blinked a few times.

"Did you hear me, Jake? I said I saw a ghost."

"Yes, I heard you. A ghost. Was it Mr. Edmund?"

The question stunned her. The words strangled in her throat. "How did you know?"

He stood and poured another glass of milk. "I've seen him before."

Stunned, she gawked at him.

He chugged the white liquid straight down before he answered. "I figured you saw him, too. That's why you hung out in the cemetery."

"But…but."

His stoic face flashed a hint of a grin. "You thought you were the only one to see him?"

She found her voice. "Well, yes. No one else wants to talk of it. The subject of loud thumping came up, but no one mentioned they actually saw him."

Jake patted Zeke. The dog beat his tail against the floor in a happy response. "I'm not sure anyone else *has* seen him. I ain't talked to the others about what I saw."

A bit relieved at his casual demeanor, she pressed for more. "How many times?"

"Oh, only three or four times. He doesn't see me. And I've only seen him in the cemetery. Crying over Mary McAdams grave."

"But, aren't you frightened? It's a ghost, after all."

A smidgen of a smile creased his lips. "I was at first, but he doesn't notice me. I kind of got used to him. When the light appeared in the window upstairs, I figured something new happened. I remembered you were alone, thought I'd check it out."

Phebe went absently to the ice box and pulled out the roast beef and bread. "It's late. You must be hungry. Would you like a sandwich?"

"Yes, please."

Assembling the sandwich gave her time to decide how much to tell him. After all, he was only twelve. After the run-around from Winston and Myrtle, it was nice to have someone who wasn't afraid to talk about it. However, she didn't want to take advantage of a young boy's willingness to discuss the matter. She must take care.

Her back was to him as she prepared the bread. "I was told not to go up to the third floor. They said the other governesses heard thumping up there. It's why they didn't stay. Even though I was told to avoid it, I didn't listen. That's when I met him—Edmund, I mean. He appeared one night, tossing books onto the floor. He saw me, as well."

"Did he tell ya about his murder?"

She whirled around, butter knife in hand. "You know about that?"

"Yep, everyone does. My stomach is growling. That sandwich sure looks good."

"Oh, sorry." She turned back to the task. "But, why doesn't anyone talk about the murder? Why is it such a secret?" She turned back to the task.

"Some kind of scandal. Some whisper about it, but mostly people avoid it. Something to do with Mrs. Powell, I think." He grabbed the sandwich from her hand and wolfed it down.

She watched him. "My, you *were* hungry."

Still chewing, he pointed to Zeke. "You got anything for him?"

Scraps were kept in a container in the icebox to feed to the pigs outside the barn.

"I think I can scare up something."

They watched Zeke gobble the pig's bounty in silence.

Jake spoke first. "You were tellin' me how you met Edmund—er, his ghost."

"Oh, yes. I was reflecting on what you said about Mrs. Powell. What is she hiding?"

"Hiding? I don't think she's hidin' anything. Jonathan and Mary are her parents. She doesn't like to talk of them from what I hear. Mother told me Ms. Powell moved all the portraits to the library and locked the door. Not sure why. My father was assigned the task."

"The library? I was just there last night. I didn't see any portraits."

"Oh, the pictures are there, all right. If you were in the library, they must have left you a key. If you want, I'll show you." Jake stood.

Phebe retrieved the key from her dress pocket and followed the boy.

Inside, Jake went to the first portrait on the far wall. "This one is Mr. Jonathan."

The man was stylish, light brown hair, no smile, with a somber, almost petulant look. His brown eyes were hooded, as if posing for a portrait was somewhat tedious. His attire was as austere as his unremarkable countenance.

"He looks nothing like Edmund. His hair is straight as a board, Edmund's is wavy. His eyes are brown, his jaw is weak. And the nose, why it's aquiline compared to Edmund's Romanesque nose. I can't see any family resemblance."

"I wouldn't know about that. Over here is Mary."

The light revealed a young, beautiful woman. Golden hair piled atop her head in the fashion of the day, bright blue eyes, a sweet smile, and adorned in a rose lace dress, a cameo pinned at her throat.

"I can see why Edmund fell in love with her," Phebe said.

The next one made her gasp. There was no doubt the man staring back at her was Edmund. A happier, more carefree depiction, but him none-the-less. "Edmund."

Her heart skipped. Dark hair, strong jaw, the prominent nose, and those amber and green eyes. The painter captured his very soul. The happy smile made him even more handsome, if that was possible. Unlike Jonathan, his ensemble complimented both his eyes and dark hair. A forest green jacket, a deep burgundy ascot fashioned with a pin emblazoned with a crest of some kind, and an emerald pinky ring on his hand.

*He certainly had a flair for fashion. It's easy to see he was in love with Mary when that was painted. His eyes sparkle with new found love.*

There was one more picture. A baby. Only months old, but something about the portrait struck her immediately.

A gold placard said, *Anthony Maurice McAdams.* Dressed in a soft blue outfit, the child looked merry and happy. The sweet smile resembled Mary, but the eyes of green and amber were those of Edmund himself.

She held the candle closer. The eyes glowed in the dim light. Amber flecks danced as light flickered over the painting.

"This is extraordinary. Edmund, Elizabet, and this baby have the same eyes."

She moved to Jonathan's portrait and studied it again.

The next wall held more family portraits.

The first was a couple, seated side by side with a gold-plated inscription at the corner. Portia and Sigmund McAdams. By the mode of dress, she determined they must be Edmund and Jonathan's parents. The man also wore a pin emblazoned with a crest. She noted the green eyes of the woman and the annoyed look of her husband.

She moved to the next one. An auburn-haired woman, not as lovely as Mary, but handsome. "Who is she?"

"That's Ms. Lucy."

"I've not heard anyone mention her." Phebe said.

Jake answered, "She married Jonathan after Mary died, so the story goes."

Another portrait hung next to Lucy's. A young girl. Fair-haired with blue eyes, dressed in cornflower blue with the inscription *Emma Alida Powell.*

The next picture was of a small boy, about two, with

green and amber eyes, a shock of black hair, and a nose the exact duplicate of Edmund's. "Anthony again."

"Jake, Mary is buried next to Jonathan. I didn't see a grave for Lucy. What happened to her?"

"No one knows. She just disappeared."

## Chapter SIXTEEN

After Jake left, Phebe tried to make sense of things. She decided the answers were in the diary. *If I want to know, I'll have to read it.*

The private diary of Mary McAdams lay heavy in her hand.

"Edmund was upset about something in the book. *I am curious about the boy in the portrait.*"

The journal beckoned her until she opened it.

Her eyes focused on the part she'd read before. *Dear Diary. I met the most wonderful man today. His name is Edmund.*

Impatient, she let the pages flutter through her fingers, looking for the part where Jonathan confessed something.

She found it. *Dear Diary. Jonathan confessed to me today.*

Her index finger underscored the words and with a bit of trepidation, she continued.

*I'm taking the children and leaving today. He has left me*

*no choice. I won't live in a house of deceit.*

The candle sputtered on Phebe's nightstand, almost extinguished in the melted wax. The morning sun streamed through the windows, but she remained focused on the words she'd read over and over, trying to make sense of the whole thing. She flipped back to the first part, afraid she might miss something.

Mary wrote: *Edmund is dead. Nothing can comfort me. I am lost with a secret I cannot share. Oh, my love, I miss you. You didn't know. I tried to tell you, but it's too late, now.*

Phebe whispered over the diary, "How did she bear it?"

The next page described Edmund's death and Mary's anguish at the discovery.

*I found him in the sky-parlor, a broken sherry glass lay near his hand, the dark wine stained the carpet like blood. His skin was cold, his lips blue. I screamed his name.*

Phebe's head jerked up at the sound of voices floating up the stairs. Her name was called.

"Phebe, Ms. Phebe, are ya upstairs? Me and Winston are back."

She shoved the book under her pillow and rushed to the stairs. "Yes, I'm here. I'll be right down."

Her dress was wrinkled, as she hadn't changed it since yesterday morning. Hurriedly, she tucked her hair under a cotton scarf and flew down the stairs.

"My, I didn't expect you back so soon."

Myrtle looked her up and down. "Whatever have you been doing, child? You look a mess."

She reached up to touch her hair. "Oh, I was rearranging the classroom. I decided it wasn't to my liking. With the house so empty, I felt it better to stay busy. I'll run upstairs and straighten up. Will the Powell's be back soon, as well?"

Myrtle's sour look relaxed. "Well, good. It's nice to know you stayed busy. Idle hands, ya know. Yes, the family will return this afternoon. Now get along with ya. I have meals to prepare."

Mixed emotions played in her mind as she rushed upstairs. Of course, she was glad to have them back, but at the same time, their return left her no time to read more of the diary.

---

The afternoon passed quickly in preparation for the Powell's return. Phebe helped in the kitchen while Myrtle chatted about the visit with her family.

"How come you didn't tell me you were married?"

"I suppose it's because you never asked."

Phebe snorted a laugh. "You are the one who tells me I ask too many questions. Now, you're complaining because I didn't ask enough? Do you have children?"

The Powell children burst through the door, halting the conversation.

"Ms. Phebe, Ms. Phebe! We're back. I have so much to tell you. I caught a fish." Elizabet tumbled her words in excitement. "There was a boat ride, a black cat, Charley climbed the biggest tree, and —."

Mr. Powell interrupted, "Enough Elizabet." He turned to Phebe. "Take the children upstairs and get them settled with a story or something until dinner."

His disgruntled demeanor wasn't lost on her. Something hadn't gone right for him on this visit. She scooped the children with arms out-stretched and herded them upstairs, loathe to be out of earshot.

*The mysteries surrounding this family continue to grow.*

It was difficult to calm the youngsters. A weekend of running free only served to unleash their naturally wild nature. They regaled her with the adventures of the countryside, all trying to speak at once, interrupting each other with a new, more exciting story.

Finally, it was too much.

"Halt. Enough. Sit in your seats with your hands folded on your desk. I will hear one story from each of you. Five minutes at the most. Elizabet, you go first. Tell me the most favorite thing about your visit."

The little girl stood, gave her brothers a smug look, and began. "The thing I loved most was fishing. I caught a fish all by myself. Well, I had help reeling it in, but I caught it."

One by one, they tried to outdo each other with their adventures. She listened patiently.

As the dinner hour approached, Winston came to retrieve the children.

Elizabet dawdled behind her brothers. "I told the best story, didn't I, Ms. Phebe?"

She hugged the child and urged her out the door. "You told a wonderful story. Why, it was almost as if I was there."

Anxious to get back to the diary, she decided to skip dinner, confident Myrtle would leave her a plate in the icebox.

When she was sure everyone was downstairs, she

hurried to her room. The diary opened easily to the last page she'd read. The description of Mary's discovery.

*I tried to shake him, begging him to wake up, but he lay still. The room was so quiet. I screamed his name again. Winston found me bent over him. 'What happened?' he asked.' I answered, sobbing. 'I found him like this. Please tell me he's not dead.'*

As she read on, Mary explained the chaos in the wake of the tragedy. A flurry of activity, the authorities, the investigation, the funeral. All of it happening with Winston by her side.

She looked up from the page. *Winston must have been very young. Even then, he was very loyal to the family.*

She hurried through the aftermath and read on the next page. *My dearly beloved is gone. Gone before I could tell him. My position is now in jeopardy, because the devastating news will disgrace my family. I've no one to turn to. Winston has been a solid friend throughout this ordeal, but as a butler he can do little for me, now. What am I to do?*

Tears stained the next few pages as Mary lamented her plight, giving over to grief and fear. And then…a solution.

*Jonathan came to me today, pulled me out to the garden.*

*He whispered, 'I've been watching you, Mary. Yes, you're grieving, but I fear something else is bothering you. You can confide in me. I'm here to help you.'*

Phebe read on as if devouring a mystery novel.

*'Yes Jonathan, I'm afraid I am in trouble. I cannot go to my family. It has to do with—Edmund.'*

*'Are you with child, Mary?'*

*I thought I would die with shame. 'How did you know?'*

*Jonathan gripped my shoulders. 'I saw you and Edmund in the hayloft one day. It didn't take me long to realize what happened. There is only one thing to do. You must marry me. Soon.'*

Phebe whispered to the empty room. "The child is Edmund's."

# Chapter SEVENTEEN

The shock of Mary and Edmund's indiscretion left Phebe breathless. Anthony McAdams was the product of their love; Mary is trying to tell Edmund he has a son.

Possibilities abounded. *Did Jonathan kill his brother to claim Mary for his own? What happened to Anthony? Mary said she was taking the children, so a second child was born. Jonathan's child. Emma—Mrs. Powell. Did Mary discover Jonathan killed Edmund?*

The facts as Phebe saw them: younger brother, jealous of the older brother, kills him to take everything, even Mary, for himself. It was a huge scandal. *Did the whole town think Jonathan killed him? They must have. Did Jonathan confess to her?*

Edmund's ghostly appearance in the sky-parlor made perfect sense if one thought about it in the realm of the supernatural. *Mary can't rest until he knows.*

She whispered over the diary and turned the page.

"Edmund's spirit doesn't know she married his brother, nor does he know about the child. Their love is so strong the grave cannot contain it."

A knock interrupted her thoughts.

Myrtle's voice drifted through the closed door. "Phebe. You didn't come down for dinner. I've brought you something to eat. You can't keep skipping meals, my dear. It doesn't do a body good."

Phebe slammed the journal shut and stuffed it under the mattress. "Coming."

Her hand shook as she opened the door, the question ready to explode from her lips. *Where is Anthony McAdams!*

The cook bustled into the room. "What's gotten into you, young lady? Skipping meals and such. You *need* your strength to corral those children. I don't understand how you do it." She placed the tray on the bed, still chattering.

Phebe remained at the door and watched her, trying to still her erratic heartbeat.

Myrtle stopped and looked up. "What is it child? You're positively pale. Are ya ill?"

"No," Phebe whispered.

"Well, something's not right. Let me feel your forehead." She felt Phebe's cheek and brow. "No fever. Maybe you're not getting enough red meat. Now, see that you eat. And no more skipping meals." She turned half way down the hallway. "The children will be up for you to tuck them in, soon. You can bring the tray down to the kitchen then."

She stifled the question she wanted to scream, '*What happened to Anthony McAdams!*'

The aroma of hot biscuits and honey tickled her nose.

"She's right in one respect. I need to eat if I'm to continue searching out this mystery. I'll need strength for the late-night visits with Edmund. *If* he returns."

Myrtle was a marvelous cook; however, she could only pick at the biscuits and honey, stab her fork at the slab of pork roast, turn her nose at the steamed green beans, but she smiled at the side dish of sliced apples. "*That* I can eat."

As she savored the last bite of apple, the children clattered up the stairs, calling her name, shouting over one another.

She pulled the door open. "Children! That will be enough."

Charley hurried in front of the others. "I want to be tucked in first tonight." He crossed his arms and his bottom lip protruded.

"Now, Charley, you know we do things in order. It's Benjamin's turn to be first. Your turn is tomorrow night."

Benjamin pushed his brother out of the way and took her hand. As a last jab at Charley, he stuck his tongue out.

Charley wailed.

"Benjamin, a gesture like that is totally unacceptable. You have forfeited your turn. You are brothers. You must look out for one another, not indulge in such divisive behavior." She dropped Benjamin's hand.

Elizabet stepped forward with a sweet smile and asked, "May I have my turn first tonight? Both the boys have been so naughty."

"No, it's not fair," Benjamin shouted.

Exasperated at the wild behavior the children displayed since their return from the trip, she made a snap decision.

"You will all tuck yourselves in tonight without me. When you can learn to be respectful and take your proper turns, we will discuss the matter. Until then, I will not come to your rooms before bedtime. You all have books on your shelves. Please read a short story to yourselves and prepare to give a report in class tomorrow."

Elizabet protested, "But I didn't…"

She pointed to the bedroom doors. "All three of you have been naughty since your return. We must restore order."

"Yes, Ms. Phebe," they said in unison.

Each door closed softly.

Fifteen minutes passed.

She went to each child's room, knocked softly and peeked inside to make sure they were tucked in, reading a story. "Bad behavior will not be rewarded," she told them. "Give respect and respect will be given in return."

When the children were settled, she returned to her room and stood at the window. The stars shined bright, twinkling as if in amusement. "I don't know what happened on that trip this weekend, but Myrtle said I'd be expected to go along the next time. Maybe I'll find out why they become so rowdy after a visit with their aunt."

The need to read more of the diary pulled her back to the present, but when she turned toward the bed, she saw the dinner tray. "Oh, I need to take it down to the kitchen. The diary will have to wait."

As she approached the last few steps to the kitchen, she heard her name and held her breath.

Myrtle's hushed voice continued. "Phebe doesn't look

well. Not ill exactly, but like something is bothering her. Strained, you know what I mean? I didn't like leaving her alone in this house all weekend."

Phebe's heart raced.

Winston answered, "I was of the same opinion. She's barely been here a week. It wasn't right to leave her alone."

"What if the noises overwhelmed her? What if she went snooping?"

The tray wobbled in her hands, the silverware clattered against the china plate. *Caught!* She hurried down the last few stairs and tried to act as if she hadn't been eavesdropping. "What are you two whispering about? It's not like you to be up so late. Are you telling ghost stories without me?"

Myrtle's face blanched.

Winston coughed.

"You both look guilty. If it's juicy gossip, I'd love to hear it."

"Nothing to concern you, dear. You have enough to worry about. I was just going to bed." She went over to take the tray from Phebe.

"No, no, I'll clean up. You work too hard."

"Well, all right. I'll let you clean up…this time." Myrtle went toward the room on the end of the kitchen and turned. "See you in the morning, then. Make sure you come down to breakfast. I'm making blueberry pancakes."

Phebe nodded, turned to Winston and nearly choked. Flickering in the glow of the gaslight was an emerald ring, securely ensconced on Winston's right-hand pinky. It was impossible for her to tear her eyes away. She feigned a fit of coughing.

Winston stood. "Are you quite all right, my dear? Anything I can do?"

She set the tray on the table. "No, no, I'm fine. Just a dry throat. I believe I'll have a hot cup of coffee. Care to join me?"

He shook his head. "Coffee keeps me up at night. I'll say good night, now."

Alone in the kitchen, she busied herself with the clean-up and thought about the strange events. *I wish I could get a closer look at that ring. I know it's the same one Edmund wore in the portrait. How did it come to be on Winston's hand? And why were they so concerned about me snooping around in the house. I'm going up to tell Edmund about his son, tonight. I'll ask about the ring. I hope he shows up.*

## Chapter EIGHTEEN

Phebe rocked back and forth in the sky parlor staring at the discovery she made near the window, all thoughts of the emerald ring gone as she stared at the floor. A red stain on the flat weave carpet. She never noticed it before. It raised the hair on the back of her neck. *It's either a wine stain or—blood. Edmund's?*

She rocked faster and faster trying to convince herself it was the wine stain. *Edmund dropped the glass as he became ill. I've heard some poisons cause a person to bleed from the mouth, so it could be blood. Still, no one knew for sure what killed him. It might have been a blow on the head. Another accounting for blood.*

The rocker stopped, and she stood. "What am I saying? Myrtle said the doctor thought it was his heart. *She* suggested poison. No one said anything about a murder weapon or injury. Why would she bring up poison? It's sure she knows more than she's telling me."

Myrtle told her about the sherry glass when she first

arrived at the house. *Mary* talked about the stain in her diary. Now, it was real, right in front of her.

She addressed the empty room as she paced. "I've been up here a dozen times. Why didn't I see it before?" Her fingers slid over the smooth tabletop; the toe of her shoe ran across the carpet. "Because I expected it to be near the table, I suppose. The decanter is there, the sherry glasses. I presumed he fell near the table after drinking the wine, but no stain darkens the carpet there." She crossed to the window. "Was he looking out at the lawns when he died? Or was he looking at Jonathan?" Now, she whispered, "Please come back Edmund."

The diary fell open to the last page she read. It told of the discreet marriage ceremony, held in the library, with only Jonathan and Mary's parents in attendance. And the parson, of course.

*'The ceremony was short. I don't remember much of it except for the bewildered looks from Mother and Father at the sudden decision. They must have suspected, because their faces looked so sad. Jonathan's parents, however, beamed their approval of the match.'*

Phebe's heart wrenched at how Jonathan whisked her away on a honeymoon trip, designed to keep them away until the birth of the child.

*'I am mourning for Edmund, but Jonathan insists on exercising his husbandly rights. He argues it will make it more plausible that the child is his, at least in his mind. I have no choice. He rescued my child and myself. It is all I can do to let him touch me. He isn't tender or loving, but rough, as if anger consumes him. Above everything, he wants this child to be*

*his, to erase any part of Edmund from my memory.'*

"The cad!" She slammed the book shut. "How can he treat Mary so? I dislike him intensely, even though he saved Mary from a life of disgrace."

When her breathing slowed, she re-opened the diary and read on.

*'Time is drawing near for the child's arrival. We must travel home or risk giving birth on the highway or at some inn along the way. The trip is difficult, but we will be home in plenty of time.'*

Next entry: *'Home, at last. I am writing this settled in my old room surrounded by the many gifts friends have brought for the baby. Jonathan's parents made the announcement.*

Phebe skimmed over the account of the days of confinement and reached the day of the birth.

*'He's beautiful. A shock of black hair, Edmund's strong jaw, and his eyes, why they are exactly like Edmund's. I've named him Anthony.'*

The clock struck eleven p.m. The house was quiet.

She closed the book and hid it in the folds of her skirt. *Please come tonight, Edmund. I have so much to tell you.*

The minutes ticked by. If he didn't show himself soon, it could mean he's gone forever. *But, it doesn't make sense! Mary wants him to know of the son she bore him.*

A glow appeared near the window.

"Edmund is that you? Please show yourself. I have news."

While she watched, he appeared as before.

"Hello, Phebe."

"Well, at least you remembered my name this time.

Where have you been?"

"I told you. I have no control over when I come and go." He looked down at the book in her lap. "You still have the diary."

"Of course."

"Have you read it?"

She stood. "Parts of it. I only did it because you weren't around. You should be the one reading it."

"What have you learned?"

"No, I shouldn't be the one to tell you." She laid it on the table and opened to the place where Mary revealed Anthony. "Read it, find out for yourself by Mary's hand."

He stepped toward her. "I have read some of it. It's why I disappeared."

"You said it was something more sinister, and then, you were gone. What was it you read?"

"It wasn't Jonathan who killed me."

Phebe couldn't get her mouth to work. It flopped open and shut. She thought of the confession Mary spoke of, assumed it meant Jonathan told her what he did. When she finally recovered, she asked, "It wasn't Jonathan? Then who?"

He faded a bit. "Mary wants me to read the diary. There's something else she desperately wants me to know. Do you know what it is?"

"What? Something else? What could be more important than who killed you?"

"Mary has a message of importance for me. Will you keep it from me?"

Phebe released the breath she'd been holding, hoping to find out who killed Edmund, but she realized Mary's message about their son was not delivered. "Of course, you're right. There's news you should know." She pointed to the passage of interest.

He shook his head. "No, I can't bare seeing Mary's handwriting. It's so beautiful, like her. It increases my sadness immeasurably. You've read it. Please tell me what she wants me to know."

Phebe marveled at this profound turn of events. *I came to this house to be governess to three small children and find myself talking to a ghost. I stand between two realms as a messenger for a mystery that happened long ago. It's impossible to comprehend, but if he wants me to tell him. I have no choice.*

"You have a son."

As much as an apparition can, he trembled. The light around his body turned into a kaleidoscope of pulsating colors. An overwhelming sense of happiness filled the room and Phebe basked in the joy-filled atmosphere.

"A son," he whispered.

"Yes, his name is Anthony."

Several minutes of silence passed as the light continued to dance and play around the room. It was like a celebration.

Finally, the resplendent glow receded.

Edmund sat down in the chair. "I never knew it. Mary didn't tell me."

"It's all in the diary. Do you remember she wanted to reveal something just before your wedding day, but your brother interrupted?"

"Yes, I remember. I was murdered shortly after. Is this what she wanted to tell me? She was with child?"

"Yes."

"And I left her." He bowed his head. "I left her to deal with the scandal alone."

"No, Edmund. You were murdered. It wasn't your fault."

He looked at her, eyes tortured. "It *was* my fault. My indiscretion. I can never forgive myself."

As Phebe reached to comfort him the room took on a different light.

Edmund looked up and stared past her.

She glanced around the room, but saw nothing.

"Mary, is that you?" Edmund stood and took a step.

"What is it, Edmund? What do you see?"

"It's Mary, after all this time, I can finally see her."

Phebe stood and whirled around. "I don't see her, where is she?"

He whispered, "She's right beside me. My beautiful Mary."

# Chapter NINETEEN

Phebe watched as Edmund faded from the room.

"No! Don't go. I don't know who murdered you."

But, he was gone.

She remained motionless while disbelief riddled any expectation of normalcy. "Mary was here, but I didn't see her. How is it I can see Edmund, but not Mary?"

She paced back and forth, looking for something, anything to explain what just happened.

The room offered no clues.

Suddenly, doubt crept into her thoughts. The appearance of Edmund, at first, left her excited as well as intrigued and occupied her thoughts daily. But something different was happening now. She didn't like it. "One ghost maybe, but another I can't see? She hurried to the door. "I must leave this room before a whole host of dead McAdams appear or rather *not* appear. Oh, what am I saying?"

The journal lay open on the table. She closed it with a

bang and left the room, intent on leaving the book and the ghost behind. "I won't come back here. It's over. Mary and Edmund are together. That was the goal. Now it's time for my interference to end."

---

Tears stained her cheeks as she struggled to awaken the next morning. Sleep did not come easy last night as she wrestled with dark figures floating through her dreams, sparking fear and trepidation.

It was hard to dress, to arrange her hair. She moved in slow motion, dreading the day with the children.

"This isn't like me. I love children. I love this job." She shrugged. "Maybe a hot breakfast will restore my spirit."

The kitchen was quiet.

Myrtle stirred a pot on the stove, curls of steam licked her face as they curled to the ceiling.

Winston busied himself with the arrangement of the breakfast tray for Mr. and Mrs. Powell.

Myrtle greeted her, "Good morning, Phebe. Hope you slept well."

She opened her mouth, but was distracted by a stab of green light in the morning sun. Its brilliance blinded her. An emerald on Winston's hand shot shards of green light in the morning sun.

*The ring! I completely forgot.*

"Something wrong, dear?" Myrtle asked.

"What? No. The light…it blinded me for a moment." She stared at Winston's hand.

Myrtle dropped the spoon and rushed to her side. "Why you're positively pale, Phebe. Should we send for a doctor?"

"Please. No doctor. I didn't sleep well, that's all. I'll be right as rain after some of your blueberry pancakes."

Winston flushed at Phebe's intense gaze. "You're staring, again. Is something amiss?"

"Your ring. Is it new? I don't believe I've seen you wear it before."

He tucked his hand behind his back, a rare blush staining his cheeks. "The ring? No, not new, a gift. I forgot to remove it."

"A gift? What a special gift. A family heirloom, perhaps?"

He stood straighter and frowned, the blush changed from light pink to a foreboding deeper red. "May I remind you of your station here, Ms. Whiteside. You are the governess and its improper for you to continuously ask intimate questions of the staff or the children. I suggest you adjust your behavior accordingly." He stomped from the room.

Myrtle's grip tightened on her arm. "Sit down, Phebe. You look as if you are about to faint."

She sank into the chair next the table. "Why's he so angry? It's a beautiful ring. I'm merely curious."

"Winston takes his job of overseeing the family very seriously. Preserving their privacy is his number one priority. Ever since you arrived, you continue to ask questions. It's unbecoming. I think we've indulged you because this is a new employment. But you must curb your bent toward curiosity and understand your place here." She patted Phebe's hand and returned to the stove.

"But, the ring. I've seen it before."

Myrtle swiveled to face her, lips pressed into a fine line, eyes narrowed. "I strongly suggest you forget about that ring—if you want to keep your position here."

The air in the room chilled by several degrees when the veiled threat was issued. Suddenly, she was afraid. Whatever was going on in this house was more sinister than first imagined.

Myrtle placed a stack of pancakes in front of her. "Now, eat."

"Yes, ma'am," she whispered.

The two women didn't speak further.

*I think I might have lost a friend this morning.* She finished her breakfast, washed and dried her plate, placed it back in the cupboard, and climbed the stairs to the classroom.

---

The children challenged her physical ability all morning. Lack of sleep and the encounter in the kitchen jarred her focus. As noon approached, she yearned for the quiet of her room and the comfort of her bed. The afternoon class would prove impossible without a short nap.

Winston came to gather the children without a word or a glance in her direction.

She did notice the ring was gone from his hand. "Good, no more thoughts of Edmund and murder, no more Mary, no midnight excursions to the third floor, and no more ring. From now on, I concentrate only on the children and their lessons."

The intent to skip the noon meal gave her pause. On the one hand, it allowed her time to recuperate, on the other, she risked Myrtle bringing a tray to her room. "Although, she's quite upset with me, so she might think better of it. At any rate, I need a bit of rest if I'm to continue today."

The decision made, she marched to her room determined to rest undisturbed. The lock made a satisfying click, reassurance her sanctuary was secured. A deep breath cleansed the morning's chaos from her mind as she rid her sore feet of the cumbersome shoes and stretched out on the bed. "Just a few winks and I'll be ready to face the afternoon."

A last plump of the pillow and she escaped into a peaceful slumber.

An unusual sensation woke her. Nothing tangible, *just something*. She turned and tucked her hand under the pillow and came wide awake as her hand brushed something hard. She flung the pillow aside and snatched her hand back as if a snake lay coiled, ready to strike. She stared in disbelief.

*Mary's journal.*

# Chapter TWENTY

Phebe wasn't easily rattled. In fact, she prided herself on facing hardship or challenges with squared shoulders and a thrust of her chin. But this...this left her shaken.

"I know I left the journal upstairs. I even slammed it shut on the table. How did it get *here*? Under my pillow, no less."

Like a lion crouched in retreat against an aggressive foe, she eased away from the journal and off the bed. She couldn't stop staring. The book taunted her, the vibrations from it palpable. It was inanimate, of course, but she expected it to rise in the air and sail toward her at any moment.

She shook her head. "No. I made my decision last night. No more ghosts. No journals. No mystery. Whatever happened upstairs I'm determined to put aside now.

Her nerves receded a bit at the decision, but the book still lay there. How would she dispose of it?

A knock on the door made her jump.

"Phebe, it's me. I brought you a sandwich. Please, you must eat."

Panicked Cook might see the journal, she flung the pillow over the top of it and jumped back, unwilling to make more contact than necessary.

"Yes, I'm coming."

Myrtle held the tray with wide eyes and a contrite, lopsided smile. "May I come in for a second?"

Phebe drew the door wide, cautious of an oncoming tirade. "Certainly." She watched the cook set the tray on the table.

Myrtle wiped her hands on her apron, nervously. "Phebe, I…I want to apologize for my abruptness this morning. I shouldn't have spoken to you in that manner."

"No, you're right. It's not my business. I'm too nosy for my own good. Please, don't fret about it. I will make every effort to concentrate on my job and not let my imagination run away with me." She paced around the room, willing her to leave.

The cook spoke, her voice soft and caring, "Child, it's only…this old house holds many secrets. Very old secrets. I suppose Winston and I are part of the fabric woven throughout this family as we've been here since we can remember. As an outsider, you simply wouldn't understand. Anyway, please forgive me for my harshness. I hope you'll continue to join Winston and I for meals. We do enjoy your company."

Myrtle left and closed the door behind her.

Phebe rushed to secure the lock.

Hunger got the best of her as the savory aroma of ham

and warm bread filled the room.

While she ate she watched the pillow, half afraid the journal would crawl out from under it. "I have to do something with it. How will I ever sleep with it in this room?"

The meal finished, it was time to go back to the classroom. She chose to leave the journal under the pillow and decide what to do with it later.

---

All three children filed into the classroom eager to resume their lessons. It gave her spirits a boost to see how they adapted to her style of teaching. The boys treated her with a new respect after the little ruckus on their return from visiting the aunt.

Elizabet looked a bit out of sorts, however.

Phebe bent over her at the desk and whispered in her ear. "Are you feeling okay, Elizabet? Your face is flushed."

The child looked up without a smile. "I didn't sleep very good last night."

"Oh, and why is that?"

"I'm not sure. Something woke me up. I had trouble falling asleep again."

Her heart lurched, her mind going immediately to the events of last night. *Did Elizabet hear something?*

Phebe decided to address her statement directly. "Did you get cold, perhaps? I wasn't there to tuck the covers under your chin. If that is what happened, I apologize. It won't happen again. You three were out of hand, you know. Discipline was in order."

"No, I wasn't cold. Something brushed my cheek and woke me up."

"Oh, a little moth, maybe. It's that time of year, you know, they…"

Elizabet placed her hand on her cheek and said in an unusually soft voice, "It wasn't a moth. It was a kiss."

She stared at the girl. "A kiss? Maybe it was a dream." Her hands turned clammy as her imagination went immediately to Edmund and Mary. *Could they—?*

"It wasn't a dream. It was a lady." Elizabet bent her head back to the book in front of her.

At the child's matter-of-fact statement, Phebe froze, unable to respond, wanting to press for more, knowing she could not. Instead, she bent close to Elizabet's ear and whispered, "We'll talk after class, dear."

Elizabet sat still, silky dark curls hiding her face.

Reluctant to resume class, she did the only thing she could do—walk away and start lessons.

---

After class, the boys rushed out of the room eager, she supposed, to get back to whatever mischief boys get into at that age.

Elizabet tried to follow suit.

"Wait, Elizabet. I'd like to talk to you." Phebe sat down behind desk. "Suppose you tell me what happened last night."

The girl stopped in the doorway and turned. "My grandparents came to visit me, that's all."

# Chapter TWENTY-ONE

Try as she might, Phebe couldn't concentrate on the words coming from Elizabet's mouth. The child's lips moved, but the only thing her brain could comprehend were the words, *my grandparents came to visit me.*

"Ms. Phebe, did you hear what I said?"

"What? Oh yes. I heard you." Her shoulders straightened, and she put on her most practical mantle. "I know you *think* you were awake, but sometimes dreams are so vivid they appear real. For example, how could you know it was your grandparents? They died before you were born. You've never met them."

Elizabet rolled her eyes with an impatient sigh. "*Because*, they told me!"

The regular rhythm of her heart stopped and took on a wild, erratic clatter. *Maybe I didn't hear her right.* "They talked to you?"

"Well, no. I didn't *hear* them talk."

"Then how…?"

The amber flecks in Elizabet's eyes glowed. "It *was* them."

"Okay, that's enough for today, little one. Let's talk about this tomorrow when you've had a good night's sleep." She put her arms around her. "Now, go find your brothers."

The little girl nodded. "Will you come and tuck me in tonight?"

"Of course, I will. Have a nice dinner with your parents. I'll see you at bed time."

Reluctant to let her go, she watched Elizabet walk out of the schoolroom.

*Is it true? Edmund and Mary appeared to little Elizabet?* She paced the classroom floor. *I wanted to leave this ghost thing behind me. Now Elizabet thinks she's seen them. How is that possible?*

"Ms. Phebe…" Elizabet returned with a smile shining on her face. "Grandfather…I know he's who you went upstairs to visit that night. Now we share a secret. Just between us girls. Promise you won't tell." She put a finger to her lips.

Before she could respond, Elizabet skipped away again.

She didn't know how long she sat there, frozen. Elizabet appeared unaffected by whatever or whomever she saw last night. Now, the child wanted to keep it a secret.

Her resolve to let the supernatural intrigue go started to crumble. *Elizabet is involved now. The so-called appearance might end her natural curiosity or spark it even more. Only time will tell. I refuse to go upstairs again, so it's imperative I find a better hiding place for the diary.*

Back in her bedroom, she tried to *will* the diary gone,

praying its appearance was only an aftermath of an overactive imagination. But, when she lifted the pillow, it lay there mocking her.

She picked it up. It tingled in her hand.

*This isn't over. It won't be over until I find out who killed Edmund. They've come to Elizabet, it's possible they will come again. But, why? So she'll know the truth? She's only five years old. How will she ever understand all of this?*

She turned it over, back and forth, trying to decide what to do. Finally, she sat down and opened it to the last page she'd read. It told of Anthony's birth.

'*This child is my first, my everything. It is all I have left of Edmund.*'

Phebe skimmed over this part, hoping to reveal more of Jonathan's confession. Finally, she stopped. *There it is.*

'*Jonathan confessed to me today. He wants another child. Soon. He doesn't pay any attention to Anthony. Avoids him at every turn. Looks away when he's brought into the room. Never visits the nursery. I know what he's thinking. Anthony is Edmund's child. He'll never forget that. Anthony is not yet a year old, but Jonathan is insisting. I don't want to bring another child into this loveless marriage.*'

She looked up as tears stung her eyes. "Poor Mary." The pages swam before her eyes as she skimmed through the hard parts. Jonathan wouldn't take no for an answer and came to her every night until it was confirmed she was with child again. Mary told of a difficult confinement and the day little Emma was born. "Elizabet's mother," Phebe murmured.

She continued reading. '*I barely see the baby. She was*

*whisked away from me shortly after birth. A governess is assigned to the nursery. I'm encouraged to let her perform all the tasks I took such joy in lavishing on Anthony. I miss that. Emma's birth left me weak. I have no strength to fight. Now that she's here, I never see Jonathan. He spends all his time with the baby. At least, I have Anthony. Even though they do their best to keep me from Emma, their interest in Anthony is minimal. I see the writing on the wall. When I get my strength back, I must take my children and leave this place.'*

"So, this is why the trunk was packed upstairs. Mary was leaving. But, she didn't. Her things are still in her room, neatly packed. What happened, why didn't she leave?"

She turned back to the diary. The next entry was short and terrifying.

*'I heard the lock click on my bedroom door late last night. I eased out of bed and tried to open it. They locked me in! But why? Where is my dear Anthony? My strength hasn't returned. I'm still very weak. I suspect they're putting something in my food. I was able to stand long enough to go to the window and look down on the front lawn. Jonathan held Emma while his parents and the governess got into the carriage. What is the governess's name? I can't seem to remember. Their formal clothes suggest a trip to church. Is this Sunday? Where is my little Anthony?'*

Phebe flipped to the next page. It was blank. She shuffled through the rest of the pages. All empty. This was Mary's last entry. "What happened to her?"

A sudden chill settled over the room as she focused on the date of the entry. *May 5, 1819.* The day was eerily familiar. She sprang from the bed, tucked the diary under the pillow, and grabbed her cloak.

Downstairs, Myrtle stopped her at the door. "What on earth are you doing? Why it's almost dark. You can't be wandering out alone at night."

"I'm just going to the stables to knock the cobwebs from my head. The horses give me such joy. I won't be long." She flashed her a smile and scurried out the door.

Jake was home by now, so no fear of running into him. She made a straight line to the stables, ducked inside, and hurried to the back of the barn. The single door opened easily as she slipped through it and out into the night.

Darkness was falling fast, but twilight couldn't deter her from the mission to confirm her suspicions.

The hinges on the old gate creaked, giving the dusky evening a surreal atmosphere. But, she wasn't afraid. Edmund was her friend, she had no fear of him. In fact, she hoped he *would* appear.

She picked her way through the tombstones, confident of the way. Mary's grave came into view. By now, the sun was gone, and a dim moon lurked behind a cloud. She could barely make out the markings on the granite. *May 7, 1819.*

## Chapter TWENTY-TWO

Phebe's knees gave way. She sank onto the damp, lush grass as the date on the tombstone danced before her eyes, distorted by a flood of tears.

*Mary died two days after the last entry in her diary.*

Unbridled emotion was not a natural trait for her. She wondered at its sudden appearance, filling her chest with sadness to the point of bursting for a woman she never met.

Alone in the peaceful cemetery, she let the tears fall, mourning Mary's untimely demise. A faint whiff of jasmine caressed her senses, cloaking her with an aura of calm in the cool beauty of the night.

After a while, questions replaced the anguish. *Why did she die so suddenly?*

One by one, she thought of the passages she read in the journal. They kept Emma from Mary, she grew weaker every day. Even Anthony's visits were limited in the end. They locked her in the bedroom and two days from her last entry, she was dead. Something didn't add up.

Finally, the cold ground seeped through her clothes. A shiver shook her body as she stood. As she prepared to leave, she lightly traced her fingers across Mary's name engraved on the tombstone. "Both you and Edmund died mysteriously. I can't leave it alone. I must find out what happened. Not to assuage my own curiosity, but for Elizabet."

The night wrapped her in darkness, the narrow lane barely visible. The horses whinnied softly when she entered the barn. At every stall, she stopped to caress each horse's velvety muzzle.

Time stood still in the cemetery, now she worried she'd been gone too long. "I'll get a tongue lashing, no doubt. But, you'll back me up, won't you, Rowena?" She rubbed the beautiful bay's nose while it snuffled her sleeve. "No carrots today. I'll bring double tomorrow."

After a last pat, she squared her shoulders and prepared to face the consequences.

As suspected, the cook stood at the stove, wooden spoon in hand.

"And just where have you been, young lady? It's unseemly for you to wander around in the dark. Why, what will people say?"

"I'm not a child. I spent some time with the horses. You needn't worry."

Myrtle flushed, two little spots of pink adorned her cheeks. "Well…it's just…why, you haven't had any supper."

"You're right! And I'm starved. Is it too late for me to have a bowl of whatever smells so good?"

Always vain about her cooking, it was easy to distract her from the point at hand. "Never too late for a good meal.

Sit down, I'll dish it up."

Constant sideway glances and throat clearings from the cook prompted her to ask, "Something on your mind, Myrtle?"

"Well, no, I mean, it's Miss Elizabet. Her mother mentioned the child was quieter than normal today. Smiled to herself a lot. Did you notice it? Elizabet is much more mischievous than the boys. Seems out of character. I'd think she might be ill, except for the smiling."

It was hard not to choke on the bite she just swallowed, but hid her surprise rather deftly. "Why no, I've noticed no difference. She *is* almost six, maybe she's growing up a bit."

"Maybe…"

"I wouldn't worry about it. Stages, you know." She stood. "As always, supper was wonderful. I'm rather tired and still need to finish my lesson plan for tomorrow. See you in the morning."

She didn't pause for acknowledgement.

---

The diary was where she left it.

Tears welled again as she flipped it open and read the last line. *Where is my little Anthony?*

"There are no more clues to be found," she said to the empty room. "The journal has left me more questions than before. Now, there are two deaths to figure out. Edmund's *and* Mary's. I promised myself I wouldn't pursue this any longer, but little Elizabet is involved now."

She snapped the journal shut and stood. "There is only

one person who can give me more information. Anthony."

A risky idea formed while she paced the room. *I can't ask Elizabet, but maybe someone in town would know something. It's time I made a trip to the market myself. There are people who must know what happened to him.*

---

Elizabet didn't mention the appearance of her grandparents during the next day's lessons. Phebe was content to leave it that way.

A daring thought niggled at her during class. Every few minutes, she glanced at the small clock on the wall, anticipating the end of the school day. Finally, the chime indicated class was over. She was free to pursue the intriguing idea of gleaning more clues about the illusive Anthony.

Part of her plan included Winston. A candid explanation would show an innocent intent. He wouldn't expect that.

All three children left the class room with a book in hand to read and discuss on the next day.

If she was to catch Winston, she must hurry.

He was in the dining room inspecting the silver.

"Hello, Winston. It's a fine day, isn't it?"

A quick glance was his only response as he held a silver table knife to the window light for any sign of a smudge.

"I'd like to take a buggy into town, if it's all right. I wasn't sure who to ask. I'm an experienced driver, so you needn't worry. I'm sure Jake would prepare one for me." She held her breath awaiting his reaction.

"And why do you feel the need to go into town? Don't we provide everything you need?" His eyes remained on the silver flatware shining in the window's light.

"Of course, you do. It's a lovely day. I'd like to see the town. I need a little diversion. Surely you won't begrudge me that."

He placed the utensil into the cabinet drawer and slowly turned to look at her. "We begrudge you nothing here. If you want to drive into town, then do so. You're free to come and go as you please, as long as you take care of your duties properly."

His dispassionate demeanor sent a chill down her spine. A sort of smirk played on his lips, his eyes narrowed, as if in warning.

She shrugged it off. *My imagination, again.*

"Thank you, Winston. I shouldn't be long. A drive on a day like today is just what I need."

Before she exited the room, she glanced back. He didn't move, just stared at her with an unpleasant gleam in his eyes.

*What in the world is wrong with him? He's been unpleasant since the day I noticed the emerald ring on his finger. I don't trust him. Or is it that he doesn't trust me?*

Myrtle wasn't in the kitchen and she sighed with relief.

Jake was in the barn and smiled when she entered. "Hello, Ms. Phebe. It's good to see you. What brings you to the barn?"

"I thought I might take one of the buggies and ride into town. I haven't explored much there and it's such a beautiful day. Could you get one ready for me?"

Jake straightened. "Well, I don't know. It's highly irregular for a woman to go into town unaccompanied."

"I've already mentioned it to Winston. He didn't seem to mind."

He scratched the cowlick on the top of his head. "Winston doesn't run the stables. He runs the house. Any mistakes with the horses will be on my head. I don't know if I like taking on that responsibility."

She sighed and looked around the barn. "It looks like your work is done. Why don't you come with me?"

"Me? Come with *you*?"

"Yes, it's a grand idea. A proper chaperone. If you behave, there might be a stick of candy in it for you."

He stood still, blinking as the sun's rays filtered through the dirty window over the back door.

"Well, yes or no, Jake? I don't have all day."

"I guess it wouldn't hurt. Mother is working at the Olsen's today. Won't be home 'til late. Sure, I'll drive ya."

She was glad he decided to come along. His company always cheered her up.

Together, they hooked Rowena to the older black buggy, laughing as Phebe struggled with the breast strap.

"It's been a while since I've hitched up a horse," she said.

"Here, let me do it. It's faster that way." He grinned at her as he took the straps.

Before long, they were on the road to town.

"What's got you so all fired up to get into town today?" Jake slapped the reins gently over Rowena's back.

"Nothing in particular. Just want to look around. Meet

some of the locals. I think it's time I got acquainted with the townspeople, don't you?"

The smile dimmed from his face. "I guess it's okay, but I'll remind you, people around these parts keep to themselves, pretty much."

"Don't worry, I'm all finished with the ghosts of Queens Court Acres."

He glanced sideways at her. "Good. No good comes from being nosy."

They rode in silence until the outskirts of the town came into view.

"What businesses preside in the town, Jake? Is there a general store?"

"There's a mercantile, a blacksmith, a small hotel, a post office, the doc's office, and a saloon. There's even a dress shop. You know, where a lady can get fit for a new dress. My mother used to work there. There's a few other shops, but that's about it. Oh, and the church."

She smiled. "You know it occurs to me I haven't met your mother. I need to call on her."

"Nah, she ain't much on company. Works and keeps to herself ever since Pa died."

Phebe continued to watch the town as the buildings became more defined. She saw Main Street and noticed there was quite a bustle of people on the sidewalks.

"Looks bigger than you described it, Jake. Quite a town."

"I guess. I don't come here much." He pulled up beside the hotel and hopped out to help her down.

"I'm going to find that dress shop. What will you do

while I'm gone?"

"Goin' by the blacksmith. Couple of things I need to see about."

"Meet you in an hour at the hotel? I'll buy you an ice cream."

Jake's eyes danced. "Ice cream instead of candy? Wow, that would be swell."

She watched him march off to the blacksmith, warmed at the excitement on his face. "All right, now to find the dress shop."

It didn't take long to find *Ellie's Fine Dresses*.

The little bell tinkled as she entered. The front was neat as a pin, decorated in pinks and rose colors. Very lady like and proper. Red roses adorned the large table near the window filling the room with a robust fragrance. A tea tray stood by the side window.

Two well-dressed women sat beside the tray sipping a beverage from china cups. The older of the women looked over the teacup while continuing to sip. Her eyes were bright blue and belied her age. Gray curls peeking out of a wide-brimmed bonnet was a truer measure of her age. Her blonde companion looked Phebe up and down with unabashed boldness, blinking blue eyes much like the older woman. Her bold stare took her by surprise.

"Is Ms. Ellie here?" Phebe asked.

The younger woman response bordered on rudeness. "She's in the back."

The gray-headed lady offered a softer tone. "It won't be long. She's fitting another lady."

"Thank you," Phebe said with a nod. She looked around

and chose a chair on the other side of the room.

"You must be the governess out at Queens Court Acres," the brash lady stated.

"Why yes, my name is Phebe Whiteside. May I ask your names?"

Together, the two women set their cups down and stood.

The older woman turned away. "We'll have to come back later. Other errands to run."

They left, the little bell tinkling in their wake.

"Strange," she said out loud.

"May I help you, ma'am?"

Phebe turned to see a lovely, slim woman standing in the door to the fitting room. "Yes, are you Ms. Ellie?"

"Yes," She looked around the room. "What happened to Mrs. Jameson and her daughter?"

"The women taking tea over there?" She pointed to the empty chairs. "They left, said they had other errands to do."

Ms. Ellie pushed a brown curl from her brow. "Unusual, since they insisted on an appointment today. Oh well, it's to be expected from those two. Think they own the town."

Phebe stood and extended her hand. "I'm Phebe Whiteside, the new governess at Queens Court Acres. I wanted to talk about a new dress."

Ms. Ellie laughed, a jovial, friendly laugh. "That explains it. Did you perchance tell them your name and where you worked?"

"Why yes, I did."

"Town gossips. They probably couldn't wait to tell their cronies."

"But why would they want to gossip about me? I'm nobody."

Ms. Ellie walked to the tea tray, poured a cup, and offered it to her. "Anything that goes on in that house is of interest to everyone in this town."

She took the cup from the store owner. "Then there *is* something not quite right there."

"Hasn't been right with that family for years. I hope you're being careful." Ellie poured herself a cup of hot tea.

"Well, I've been told more than once to stop asking questions." She put her cup down and looked directly at Ms. Ellie. "I don't know you, but you seem to know the history of the family. I'm looking for someone."

Ellie stood, her lovely smile gone. "I thought you came here for a dress. I have another customer in the fitting room. I really don't have time to answer—."

Phebe asked the question anyway. "Where's Anthony?"

## Chapter
## TWENTY-THREE

Phebe stood outside of *Ellie's Fine Dresses* looking around for Jake. She saw him wave at the blacksmith and head for the hotel. The sunny day didn't resonate with her anymore, dimmed by the dismal news from Ms. Ellie.

When she tried to press for more answers, Ellie's customer came out of the fitting room and put an end to the questions. Introductions were made, and Phebe made an appointment for another day to talk about the dress. She couldn't remember the lady's name because Ellie's words pounded in her head. *Anthony is dead.*

She wanted to know what happened, how old he was at the time of his death. Questions popped into her mind, one by one. All Ellie gave her was a quick whisper in her ear. *He died at two years old.*

Her leaden feet trudged toward the hotel as she returned Jake's wave. She'd promised him ice cream. It was unthinkable to disappoint him.

"Did you order a new dress?" Jake asked the question politely, but kept his eye on the hotel window.

"Actually, no. She had other customers. I'll have to go back. Ready for some ice cream?"

"Sure am!"

Inside, several customers enjoyed a dish of the cold treat. She smiled at them and watched with interest as they put heads together, whispering among themselves while their eyes remained on her.

They found a table in the corner and sat down.

"Guess everyone knows who I am by the reactions I'm getting."

Jake smiled. "Yep. I told ya. Everybody knows everybody in this town. Can I have a double scoop?"

She looked at him, his face beaming, freckles glowing. For the first time in a long time, he looked like a little boy instead of the stern, grown up, stable boy. *I wonder how long it's been since he's had a cool treat like ice cream.*

The waitress took their orders. Jake, a double scoop. She settled for a single.

The creamy goodness of vanilla slid down her throat, but she hardly noticed. Her thoughts were on Anthony's disappearance. *I never saw his grave. It should be close to Mary's.*

Every fiber within her strained to put an end to the ice cream diversion so she could hurry back to the cemetery and find Anthony's gravestone. But Jake looked so happy, she didn't have the heart to rush him.

The street outside bustled with people going about their daily missions. Phebe allowed herself the distraction of wondering where they went and what particular errand they pursued as she waited for Jake to finish. Some of the women wore expensive looking bonnets with matching parasols, but most were dressed in a more subdued homespun fashion. Several men passed by dressed in the appropriate garb of their trade. From bankers to blacksmiths and cowboys.

She looked away to ask if Jake was finished, but glanced back at the window in time to see a hatless, dark-headed man pass out of her sight. Only his back was visible, and then, he was gone. Something familiar struck her. His bearing, straight and tall, his clothes, different than the other men. Well made, expensive looking.

*Where have I seen him before?*

And then, it struck her. Edmund! *It can't be. Why on earth would he come to town? I'm simply overwrought. Seeing things that aren't there.*

She turned to hurry Jake along, but was interrupted when his spoon clattered into the empty dish.

"That was so good. Thank you, Ms. Phebe."

"You're most welcome. Ready to head home?" She took her last bite and let the spoon clatter into her bowl, as well.

They both laughed.

She paid the bill. Jake held the door for her as they stepped out into the sunshine.

The crowd on the sidewalks cleared a bit. She craned her neck in the direction the dark-haired man was headed, but saw nothing. *Just as I thought, my imagination.*

Jake helped her into the buggy and off they went.

"Anytime you need to go to town, just let me know. I'm

usually available," he said, a big smile danced on his face.

"Are you sure your offer isn't about the possibility of more ice cream?"

"Well…"

They chuckled together as Rowena trotted briskly down the trail towards home.

---

Jake led the horse into the barn and gave her a quick wave.

Her mind was still on Anthony. She turned toward the house, but waited until the barn door closed, then scurried around the old building and onto the path to the cemetery. "I must find Anthony's grave."

A light breeze carried the smell of fresh grass, soothing her jangled nerves. Her pace slowed as she breathed in the aroma. "Someone has cut the grass, recently. I wonder who keeps the cemetery grounds? I've never seen a caretaker out there? Maybe Jake does that job, too."

As she drew close to the gate, she saw a round-shouldered old man guiding some sort of contraption between the rows. He was toward the back and didn't seem to hear her approach.

Unwilling to startle him, she waited until he made a turn.

He looked up with raised brows, his lips parted as if to say something.

"Hello. I'm Phebe, the new governess here. I didn't mean to sneak up on you like that." She glanced at the contraption he was pushing. "I've never seen such a machine.

What it is?"

The old man frowned as he looked down at the mower. "Some new-fangled thing Mr. Powell bought. Says it'll make the grounds easier to maintain." He shook his head. "Rather stick to my sheep and a hoe." He scratched the top of his gray head. "Say, what are you doing out here? No one comes to this place much anymore."

"I do sometimes. It's very quiet. I like to read, and this is a good place to find some peace and quiet."

His frown returned, and his brows knit with disapproval. "Ain't no place for a young lady to wander around in. Spooky, if you ask me."

"What's your name. I told you mine. I've not seen you before."

"Elmer Evans. Not surprised old Winston didn't mention me. Sorry brother he is."

"He's your brother?!"

"Yup. We've worked for the family for forty years. Thinks he's better than me, since he's got a fancy butler job. If it weren't for me, he wouldn't even *have* that position."

"Why, I never even heard his last name. Winston Evans. Well, well."

"I gotta get back to work. It's a big cemetery." He turned back to the mower.

"Of course."

For a few minutes, she watched him mumble to himself as he tried to wrangle the new mower. Then, she remembered why she came.

Mary's gravestone shone brightly in the sun next to Jonathan's. She looked around for a child's grave marker.

There wasn't one. She checked Edmund's. Nothing.

Perplexed, she looked again, sure she missed something.

"What are you looking for?"

The old man's sudden appearance made her jump. "Uh, a grave stone. For a child."

"There ain't no child buried back here."

"You must be mistaken. I was told he died when he was two."

"I told ya. Ain't no child buried back here. I ought to know. I know these stones like the back of my hand. What name you lookin' for? Maybe it's somewhere else."

"Anthony McAdams."

Elmer's face paled under his timeworn wrinkled tan. "Anthony McAdams?"

"Yes, Mary's boy."

"I know who he is. What I don't know is why your lookin' in the cemetery."

"Where else would they bury a child of two?"

The old man sat down on a bench beside the big elm tree. "They wouldn't have buried him, at all."

Confused, Phebe watched the old man's face as his eyes moistened with tears. "I don't follow what you're saying. Of course, they would bury him."

The old man stood and took her hand. "No, no they wouldn't. Because he ain't dead."

## Chapter TWENTY-FOUR

When Elmer spoke, a cloud passed in front of the sun making his revelation even more ominous.

"Not dead? How can that be?" She returned his grip as if willing the answers from him.

"I've said too much. They got their reasons for not tellin' people, I suppose." He extracted his hand and turned away.

"Elmer, please, I have so many questions. I know it's not my business, but in some ways, it is. You see—I've seen Edmund's ghost." She didn't know what impact this revelation would have, but went with her intuition.

He stopped, but didn't turn around.

"Please, Elmer. Talk to me."

His white head shook back and forth and groaned. "I can't. I'll lose my job here. Shouldn't have told you anythin'."

"So, you've seen Edmund, too?" she asked.

Head still bowed, he answered, "No, but I've heard things."

"What things?"

He turned slowly. "No more questions. It's time for trimmin' the weeds around the gravestones. I'll run out of daylight afore it's all done. You best go home."

Instinct told her she pressed too hard. She let him go.

At the gate, she turned for a last look at the elderly man.

He waved and said, "Don't mention you talked to me. It wouldn't bode well for either of us."

"I won't tell. Take care, Elmer. Maybe I'll see you again."

Afraid she'd run into Jake before she got to the house, she hurried along the path. He would still be tending the horses, but could finish early. A sigh of relief escaped her as she slipped inside the kitchen door.

She closed the door quietly with her back to the room.

"Enjoy your day in town, Phebe?" Winston's voice was quiet.

She spun around. "Oh, I didn't see you there. You shouldn't sneak up on people like that."

"I'm sorry I startled you."

Her back straightened. She smoothed her skirt. "To answer your question, we had a lovely day. Indulged in a bit of ice cream. I met the lady at the dress shop. I enjoyed the day very much."

"Good."

"Where's Myrtle?"

"Packing."

"Really, where's she going?" She glanced around the room.

"She's packing for the children. They are going to see

their aunt in the country. By the way, you're going on this trip, too."

She blinked. "I am?"

"Yes, it's customary. The only reason you didn't go last time is that you had only just arrived."

"Oh."

Winston cleared his throat. "I suggest you go up and start packing."

"Yes, right away."

His eyes narrowed and the already prominent frown on his face deepened. But, he only nodded and left the room, leaving her to wonder at what thoughts lay behind his disapproving eyes.

Upstairs, she shut the bedroom door and stood still, staring out the window.

*I don't want to take this trip, right now. There are more questions than answers. I want to go upstairs tonight and try to find Edmund again.*

A knock on the door made her jump.

Myrtle stood in the open doorway. "Oh, there ya are, Phebe. Winston told me you were home from your trip into town. You best start packing. You're going on a special holiday with the children."

She could only stare at Myrtle.

The cook's eyes grew round. "Why, whatever is the matter, girl? I thought you'd be beside yourself to go. You're always running here and there, to the barn, to that depressing cemetery. A trip to the countryside would suit you fine."

"Nothing's wrong. I *am* excited to go. It's a surprise, that's all. I thought they only went there once a month. I don't even know what to pack."

Myrtle laughed. "Some kind of business they must attend to. Yes, your wardrobe leaves much to be desired. Same bland dresses and sensible shoes. Seems to me it wouldn't be hard at all. Just throw a couple of dresses in a suitcase and be done with it. They'll be leaving in an hour."

Phebe stood in the doorway as Myrtle descended the stairs. *An hour. Maybe I'll have time to go back to the sky-parlor.*

The suitcase closed easily as she snapped the latches shut. Two dresses, two pair of shoes, a change of undergarments, a hairbrush, and other toiletries. *Not much for a woman my age. I certainly live a simplistic life.*

The valise, a bit worn, was all she had. She scooted it into the hallway. After a quick look around, she confirmed no one was around and hurried to the stairway leading to the next floor.

Inside the parlor, she was shocked to see books strewn everywhere as if they'd flown off the shelves.

*He's back.*

Now more than ever, she wanted to stay, not accompany the family to the country. If there was a chance to talk to Edmund once more, she wanted to take it.

*Maybe I can feign illness. Surely, they won't want me to go if I have something contagious. A bad cold, influenza, whooping cough. Oh, what am I saying? No one will believe I took sick so quickly. I must make the trip and deal with Edmund when I return.*

She closed the door on the littered parlor, hurried downstairs, grabbed the suitcase, and headed for the kitchen.

## Chapter
## TWENTY-FIVE

Phebe didn't enjoy the carriage ride to the country. The children wiggled constantly, the Powell's argued about the household finances, and the road was dusty and rough. Adding to her discomfort was the memory of the parlor upstairs in disarray. *Was Edmund back or was someone else rummaging around up there?*

She stared out the window wishing she was back at Queens Court Acres.

"What world are you in, Phebe?" Mr. Powell's sharp voice cut through her musings. "I asked you a question?"

"Oh, I *am* sorry, sir. I guess I was enjoying the scenery."

He made a funny harrumph sound. "I asked if you are happy to be away from the house for a couple of days. I know your schedule with the children is hectic."

"Oh, yes indeed. It's always nice to see new places and break up one's routine occasionally."

"Good. You will no doubt accompany us on every trip

from here on out. It's nice to have someone who can occupy the children's time so Mrs. Powell and I can enjoy some leisure time with my sister."

"Of course. I'm always happy to spend time with the children."

Mrs. Powell held a scented handkerchief to her nose, but lowered it long enough to bestow a smile on her. The lacy hankie was returned to her nose post haste, however.

Phebe surmised Mrs. Powell suffered from a bit of motion sickness considering a lavender essence filled the carriage. In turn, the fragrant bouquet calmed her, as well.

An hour passed, and she wondered if they would ever arrive at their destination. The lavender faded, replaced with the odor of sweating horses mixed with the dust of the road. The children fell asleep against one another soothed by the rocking carriage. The Powell's stopped arguing and fell into a mutual silence.

*At least, calm prevails now. Hopefully, it won't be much longer.*

"Ah, here we are. Just around the corner," Mr. Powell announced.

Relieved, Phebe sat straighter, smoothed her skirt, and adjusted her bonnet in preparation of meeting the extended family.

The horses came to a stop in front of a modest farm house, well-maintained with a neatly trimmed green lawn, and a great wrap-around porch filled with bright, white rocking chairs. All in all, it was very inviting.

A woman dressed in gardening attire ran down the pathway, shears waving in gloved hands, large hat flopping.

"Children! You're here. Come, come. Let's have a glass of lemonade."

Everyone filed out of the carriage and embraced the woman.

Phebe took in the whole of Aunt Martha. Unruly gray hair peeked out from under the large brim of a straw hat. She was dressed in a tan billowing skirt with a long loose-fitting light green jacket. Piercing blue eyes sparkled with excitement. Although disheveled, there was a certain gentility about her.

Mr. Powell turned to her. "This is the new governess I told you about. Phebe Whiteside."

Phebe curtseyed. "Nice to meet you, Mrs. …"

"Just call me Martha. We don't stand on formality here. I'm so glad to meet you, finally. Robert has told me so much about you."

She blushed. "All good, I hope."

"Yes, yes, of course. Come, let's sit on the porch. I'll get Maggie to bring us some ice-cold lemonade."

Martha shed her gloves and hat and dropped them on a small table near the stairs landing. While everyone found a chair, she bustled into the house, the screen door banging shut.

The countryside was beautiful with rolling hills as far as you could see. Some trees fanned out around the grounds and a pond glistened in the distance. She noticed the well-kept garden at the side of the house and hoped she'd get a chance to explore.

Martha burst out of the front door. "Good, I'm glad everyone is settled. Maggie is bringing the refreshments. We'll visit and catch up for a bit. The children can take Phebe for a walk around the grounds, so she can stretch her legs when she feels up to it." She turned to Mrs. Powell. "Emma, I've found the most beautiful fabric. I know it will make a stunning dress for you."

Mr. Powell lit up a cigar while the ladies chatted.

The front door opened and a young girl of about twelve eased onto the porch with a large tray. The glasses rattled as she set it on the main table.

"Lemonade?"

"Why, yes, thank you." The tart liquid refreshed her instantly as she leaned back in the rocker. *Maybe this is what I needed after all. To get away and clear my head.*

While the others were served, Phebe watched the lovely young lady. Her long brown hair, tied back in a red ribbon, complimented a dewy complexion and big brown eyes.

*I wonder how she fits into this unusual family?*

The children rebounded from the long trip invigorated and eager to explore.

Elizabet tugged on her hand. "Have you rested enough? I have so much to show you. You can come with me. The boys want to ride the pony in the back."

She laughed at the child. "I suppose I am. I'm sure there are lots of things to explore around here. I'm always up for a good adventure."

Someone already removed their bags from the carriage. They sat on the bottom step.

"Let me unpack and wash my face, then we'll go exploring." The shoes she wore weren't suitable for trekking around the fields.

Elizabet frowned.

Martha swooped the girl into her arms. "Phebe is right. Let her catch her breath before you drag her off. Come into the kitchen, I've made your favorite strawberry pie. You can have a piece while we wait."

The boys clamored around Martha demanding their fair share, as well.

She stood, unexpectedly alone with the young girl, as the rest of the troop went inside.

"Uh, Maggie, isn't it?" Phebe asked.

"Yes, ma'am."

"Oh, please call me Phebe. Will you show me where I'm to stay?"

"Of course." Maggie turned to retrieve her bag.

"No, no. I can carry that. Just show me the way."

Maggie led her to a small room at the end of the upstairs hall. It was bright, sparsely furnished, but clean and inviting.

"Just come down when you're ready."

She wanted to ask Maggie more questions, but the girl hurried out the door, closing it softly.

After she brushed her hair and tied it up again, she changed shoes, and washed her face. A large window blocked only by sheer lace curtains offered a lovely view of the grounds. In fact, she could see a pond just beyond a line of trees.

She stood gazing at the serene scene. For the first time in days, a sense of peace settled over her. *This place is just what I need to calm me. I see why the family comes here so often.*

A movement in the distance caught her eyes. A flash of red. While she watched, it moved around the edge of the water. She squinted, hoping to bring it into focus.

*A man.*

Something about the way he stood, the broad shoulders, the dark hair was familiar. He held something in his hand. *A pole?*

His red shirt stood out in stark contrast to the natural scene around him.

Fascinated, she watched as he stood at the edge of the lake, drawn to him like a magnet. *I want to meet him, find out who he is and why he seems so familiar.*

She tore herself away from the window and hurried down the stairs to find the children.

"Ms. Phebe, you took forever," Elizabet said.

"I know, dear. The dust took longer to shake off then I realized. Where are your parents and the boys?"

"The boys are out with the pony and Aunt Martha. Mother and Father went to their rooms to rest. That leaves me and you."

"And Maggie? Where is she?"

"She's gone to the cabin. We'll meet her there."

"Wonderful. Then let's get on with this adventure of yours."

Elizabet pulled her down the path to the pond. She could hardly keep up with the small child. They laughed all the way until they came to a small wooden cabin just behind a stand of trees. Well hidden, she wasn't surprised she didn't see it from her bedroom window.

Voices drifted on the air, a girl and a man. As they

rounded the corner of the cabin, she hesitated. Elizabet, however, kept tugging her along. She stumbled forward at her young charges' insistence, until they came to an abrupt stop. The broad back of a man stood right in front of her wearing a red flannel shirt, the same color she saw from the upstairs window. He concentrated on baiting Maggie's fishing hook and didn't turn around.

It wasn't his confident bearing or ink black hair that arrested her breathing.

It was his voice. The familiar deep timbre rolled smoothly off his tongue.

*Edmund.*

## Chapter TWENTY-SIX

"Uncle Zig, I've brought someone to meet you," Elizabet announced.

Phebe held her breath, anxious for him to turn around, but terrified he would.

"Hold on Elizabet. You don't want me to prick Maggie's finger with this hook do you?" He remained bent to the task. "Almost got it…there!" With grand aplomb, he whirled to face her, arms flung wide. "I beg your pardon. Duty calls."

Breathless, with nothing to hold on to, both knees buckled as if her bones suddenly turned to water. She pitched forward. Blackness gobbled up the daylight as she fell, but the ticklish flannel shirt against her cheek and a stabbing pain in her left ankle rescued her from a dead faint. She wasn't unconscious, but rested in the arms of a man who looked exactly like Edmund McAdams.

"I certainly didn't mean to frighten you." He didn't move to release her, but bent toward her face, his smile twisted into an amused grin. "Let me introduce myself.

They call me Zig."

Arms flailing as if caught in a net, she extracted herself from his grasp, stood, and straightened her clothes. No amount of will power could make her look at his face. She couldn't breathe, much less speak. She bent to rub her ankle.

Elizabet saved the day. "Her heel caught in the grass. I couldn't catch her in time. This is our new governess, Ms. Phebe."

Head still angled toward the ground, she saw his hand as he extended it for a proper greeting. "Pleased to meet you Ms. Phebe. Are you all right?"

The breath re-entered her body at a feeble attempt to answer him. "I'm fine. Pardon me for my clumsiness. My ankle twisted when I tripped." She turned to Elizabet. "We should go back to the house and put a cold compress on this."

The low tone of his voice vibrated through the air around them. "There's cold water in the rain barrel. I've got a hand towel in the kitchen. No need to hike across the field. Come. This way." He grasped her arm with a firm, no nonsense grip and led her toward a small cottage.

She tried to pull back. "No, really, I need to go back to my room and lie down. I can't impose on you."

"Don't mind me if I say you look pale. The last thing you need right now is overexertion."

His hand was strong on her elbow, testament to the fact he wasn't about to take no for an answer.

The two girls hurried ahead of them.

He eased her down on a small bench outside the front

door. "Be right back."

Elizabet smiled. "Uncle Zig will fix you right up."

"I think we should go on home, I can walk…"

"Here we are. I dipped the dish towel in the rain barrel's cold water. This should make it feel better right away." He handed the cloth to Elizabet. "You may do the honors. Just wrap it around the ankle."

The towel was cold against her skin. She kept her attention on Elizabet to avoid looking at his face.

Elizabet stood and beamed at everyone. "There. All finished."

He bent to inspect her work. "Perfect. How does that feel?"

If it wasn't for the solid bench under her, she might have collapsed from his overwhelming likeness to Edmund and the voice that rolled like deep thunder.

She lifted her gaze until she met his eyes, the same amber-flecked green eyes as Edmund and Elizabet. *How can this be?*

"I'm terribly sorry. My clumsiness has inconvenienced you. Please, go on back to the lake and finish your fishing lesson with Maggie. I'll be fine here."

He raised an eye-brow. "Are you sure, then? Elizabet can stay with you until it's her turn. I hate to leave you alone. You're still pale. Wouldn't want you to faint on us."

She didn't answer him, her mind swept away with the resemblance to the ghost in the sky-parlor. The strong Romanesque nose, the square jaw. He was the spitting image of Edmund McAdams.

He continued, "Ms. Phebe? I say, maybe I shouldn't

leave you, after all. You don't seem to have your wits about you, yet."

"What? Oh no, I'm fine, really. Yes, Elizabet will stay with me."

He gave a quick salute. "All right. Coming Maggie?"

The two sprinted off to where they left the poles and bucket of bait.

She watched them; noticed his patience, his expertise with a fishing pole, the ease he displayed with the outdoors.

"Elizabet, who is Uncle Zig? Does he live at the big house or here in the cabin?"

"He's my uncle. Aunt Martha's son."

The revelation startled her. "Aunt Martha's *son*?"

"Yes, he lives out here—in the cabin. Likes to be alone except when we come to visit. Loves to fish and teach us things."

"I didn't think Aunt Martha was married."

"She isn't."

Phebe bit her tongue. So many questions popped into her head, but the child was only five years old. Too young to prod for answers.

"My ankle is much better, thanks to you. Let's go back to the house, now. I really need to lie down."

Maggie's high-pitched shriek interrupted any thoughts of leaving.

"I did it. I caught one," she shouted. The fish bounced up and down on the line as she jumped around.

Phebe's gaze left the excited Maggie and settled on Uncle Zig. His eyes lit up with joy, his smile was broad and infectious. *He's truly happy about this little fish.*

Elizabet turned to her. "May I go down and see the fish? It's my turn now. We just *can't* leave until I catch one."

"Of course. I'll be fine. Go and catch your fish."

The child scampered away without a second glance.

She leaned against the house and sighed. *My heart rate is slowing down. My wits are returning. Somehow, I'll figure this out. Meanwhile, I'll simply enjoy watching the children—and Uncle Zig.*

He glanced at her occasionally, executed a half wave as he adjusted Elizabet's pole.

She waved back and smiled.

Maggie hurried toward her, a bucket sloshing water over the sides. "Look, Ms. Phebe. I caught one. Isn't it beautiful?"

"Why yes, but whatever will you do with it?"

"Oh, we throw them back. Uncle Zig only keeps 'em if we need fish for dinner. Tonight is pot roast, so this one goes back to swim another day."

"I hardly see the purpose in this activity, then."

"It's the thrill. The skill. Uncle Zig is the best fisherman in these parts."

She smiled at the excitement on the girl's face. "I see. Does he take you fishing often?"

"Every time Mr. & Mrs. Powell bring the children. It's sort of a tradition."

"I can see all of you enjoy it very much. But, it seems odd to me that the boys don't come and fish."

Maggie frowned. "It's because Elizabet and I always catch the most fish. They don't like to lose. They have no patience."

"May I ask you a question? You don't have to answer if you don't want to."

"Of course, Ms. Phebe."

"Zig is such a peculiar name. Does it stand for Ziglar or something?"

"No, Uncle Zig is his nickname. Everyone calls him that. If you come down by the water, I'll show you why."

"No, my ankle is still sore. Why don't you simply tell me?"

"Well, it has to do with the way he wiggles the bait through the water. After he casts, he wags his pole back and forth, just a little. The bait zigs and zags. The fish are attracted to it. He's teaching me the technique." She pointed to the bucket. "I think I'm getting pretty good."

"I see. So, it's a nickname. What is his real name?"

Maggie scratched her head. "Why, I don't really know. Everyone calls him Zig. I've never thought about it. Maybe you should ask him."

The thought of asking him directly, terrified her. Deep down, she knew who he was, but to ask him and hear him say it out loud, well—she'd faint dead away for sure.

Another gleeful shriek signaled the triumphant snare of another fish.

"I caught one, I caught one," Elizabet squealed.

Phebe clapped her hands and waved.

"Let's go see, Ms. Phebe. I'll help you." Maggie offered a hand.

Hesitant, she tested her ankle. "Well, I suppose I can."

They made their way to the lake's edge, Maggie carrying her catch in the bucket.

After a complete round of exclamations and admiring inspections, Phebe paused to watch Zig's face.

He beamed with pride.

"You really enjoy this, don't you?" she asked.

"Yes, it's the highlight of the month for me. I love when the children come here."

He instructed the girls on how to release the fish and made sure both swam away, free and in good health. "I have hot tea and biscuits at the cabin. Anyone game?"

"I'm starving," Elizabet said.

"Why don't you two go on ahead and ready the refreshments. I'll assist our guest."

The two girls joined hands and raced to the cabin, squealing in anticipation.

He offered his arm. "May I?"

She hesitated, but finally, looped one arm through his, a tingle racing between them.

He looked down at her and smiled, the amber flecks in his eyes dancing with amusement. "I don't bite, Ms. Phebe."

She stopped their forward movement. "May I ask a question?"

"Sure. I'm an open book. Ask me anything."

"What's your real name? I know it's not Zig."

He threw his head back and laughed. "Oh, is that all. I thought you were going to ask me some deep, dark question by the tone of your voice. Zig is a nickname." He extracted his arm, took a deep bow and announced, "I'm Anthony. Anthony Maurice."

## Chapter TWENTY-SEVEN

Phebe's heart pounded as he said his name out loud.

*I knew it.*

Hearing his name wasn't the jolt to her system she expected. Uncle Zig was definitely Anthony Maurice McAdams. But, to make it real, she wanted to hear him say it.

He stopped and tilted his head to her in a grand gesture. "Or should I say my full name, Anthony Maurice Evans."

This time the universe stood still. She couldn't breathe. "Evans?"

"Yes. You know, I always hated my *middle* name. I have no idea how Mother came up with it. I don't think we're French. Don't you think it sounds French?" He continued to guide her toward the cabin, gently, but with purpose.

Chaos took root in her brain. "Evans?" She didn't realize she said it out loud again. Her breath came in spurts and she stumbled against him.

His grip tightened as he steadied her. "I've got you, Ms. Phebe. This uneven ground has certainly challenged you today."

They stopped in front of the cabin.

He eased her down on the bench. "Let's enjoy the refreshments. Maybe a little sustenance will restore your balance."

Maggie opened the door. "Tea is ready."

"Let's eat out here today, Maggie. Enjoy the crisp air. You can put it on the little table right there."

"Oh, it'll be fun to eat out here. We'll be right out."

After the girls settled everything on the table, he poured a cup of tea and offered it to her.

She gulped the scalding liquid, but somehow, the burning sensation restored reality. Embarrassed at her unladylike behavior, she glanced at him.

All three of her companions stood still with eyes round as she hurriedly swallowed the tea.

"I'm sorry. I believe I'm overtired from the trip. The tea is wonderful. Maybe a biscuit will bring me to full restoration. They look scrumptious."

He rushed to pick up the plate and offer her one.

Still no one spoke. All eyes remained on her.

"Please, don't look at me like I'm a two-headed cow. The country air, my sore ankle, it all has me out of sorts. I'm fine now."

"Our apologies, Ms. Phebe. It's just—the tea is so hot. Of course, you're tired. After tea and biscuits, I'll be happy to escort you to the big house." He turned to the girls. "Go on, Maggie, Elizabet, eat your biscuits. Don't be rude."

Eager to have the conversation back to normal, she asked, "Who made these? They're so light and tasty."

"Aunt Martha," the girls said in unison. "She's the *best* cook, she sent them with us in the lunch basket."

"Ah, then I will look forward to this evening's meal. Pot roast, isn't it?"

They passed the next half hour in idle chatter while she tried to make sense of his name. *Why is his last name Evans? He <u>must</u> be a McAdams.*

A fluffy, white cloud drifted in front of the sun, reminding her of the lateness of the hour.

"Really, we must get back. I'm sure Mr. and Mrs. Powell are wondering where I went. Elizabet isn't my only charge." She stood and brushed the crumbs from her dress.

"Ah, the boys are spending time with Mother and the horses. It's their habit each time they visit. The Powell's spend most of their time napping. But, you're right, rest is what you need."

The girls put away the dishes.

She noticed Zig studied her rather intently while the girls were inside. "Something wrong with my face? Crumbs? A mosquito on my nose, perhaps?"

"Excuse me for staring, Ms. Phebe, I…"

"Please," she interrupted. "Call me Phebe. After all, I've pried into your unusual name. Seems only fair."

He smiled. "Fair enough, Phebe it is. I'm only studying you because, well, for one, you're very pretty. However, you look troubled, as if a heavy weight rested on your shoulders. I hope all is well with your employment. I know for a fact the children can be quite a handful."

His discernment caught her off guard. "Oh no, everything is fine with my employers. The children are wonderful. I was at my last assignment for many years and getting to know a new way of doing things is a bit daunting, but everyone is so nice and eager to help. It already feels like home."

"We're ready, Uncle Zig." Maggie held Elizabet by the hand.

He took Phebe's elbow. "You two run ahead. I'm going to take it slow with your governess. Try to make sure she doesn't do more damage to that ankle."

They watched the children skip ahead, hand in hand.

As they strolled along, Phebe decided to probe. "Elizabet is such a firecracker. Always into mischief, loads of energy."

He didn't reply, only nodded and tightened his grip on her elbow.

They walked on.

*He was chatty enough before, but now, he's hardly said a word.*

She decided to press further. "I wonder where she got those eyes. They look very much like yours."

Still, no answer.

She tried again. "I'm sorry, did I say something wrong?"

The breeze lifted the dark locks on his brow, his eyes lost a bit of their luster, and his step slowed. "No, of course not." He stopped and faced her. "There are secrets in this family, Phebe. Secrets we are reluctant to discuss. I understand you are anxious to fit in, but in this case, I advise you to keep your curious nature to yourself. I'm not trying to be rude, but where Elizabet is concerned, I am highly protective. The truth will come to light, one day, when she's older, but for now, she needs to simply be a child."

She stared into his eyes, saw the pain, the deep concern. "I'm sorry, I…"

"No, I'm the one who's sorry. You are a smart lady. You notice things and naturally you're curious. It's better we don't discuss this any further." He took her arm again and walked on.

"You're not the first one, you know," she said.

"The first one? What do you mean?"

"Myrtle. Tells me I ask too many questions. Winston, too."

"I'm sorry, but I don't know who you are talking about."

She looked at him, wide-eyed. "The Powell's staff. Myrtle, the cook. Winston, the butler."

"Oh, of course, I remember the names, now, but I've never met them."

This time, *she* stopped. "What? How could you not? They are long-time servants. Been employed with the family for years."

He urged her to walk on. "I never go there, neither does Mother. I don't believe I've ever seen the house."

"Surely, you don't just stay here on this property? Don't you go into town?"

He laughed. "Once in a while. Don't care much for town. People stare, ask questions. I don't like it. I'm a writer. Spend my days writing for the newspapers, other publications, novels. It keeps me very busy. The only time I look up is when the children come."

"So, you are what they call a recluse."

Again, he threw back his head and laughed. "I suppose. If that's how you want to label it. I love the countryside and nature. Don't have much use for people. Of course, you are an exception."

They arrived at the front door.

"Here we are, safe and sound. I suggest you rest for the next hour. Mother will have dinner at six."

Phebe nodded. "Thank you." She hesitated. "I'm not sure what to call you now. Uncle Zig or Anthony."

"Zig will do just fine, Phebe. *Everyone* calls me Zig."

"Will you be at dinner?"

"Of course, Mother would have my head if I didn't show. Go on, now. Get some rest."

She leaned against the front door and watched him walk back toward the cabin.

In her room, the window drew her. *Just one more glance.*

Martha joined him on the path. They spoke a moment and in tandem looked up at her window. She jerked back, afraid they saw her peering down at them. When she looked again, the path was empty.

## Chapter TWENTY-EIGHT

Weary, Phebe turned from the window and settled on the bed. The whole experience at the lake unnerved her. The resemblance between Zig and Edmund was undeniable, but she overstepped by asking too many questions.

*My big mouth. Asking questions at the wrong time, to the wrong people.*

She closed her eyes and drifted off.

---

A light tap at the door woke her.

"Ms. Phebe. Dinner is in ten minutes. How's your ankle?"

It was Maggie.

She sat up and tried to get her bearings. "I'm fine. I guess I fell asleep."

Through the door, Maggie said, "If you like, I can wait

for you and help you downstairs. Wouldn't want you to injure the ankle again."

"That will be a big help. I'll be out in a moment."

Maggie's footsteps faded away.

As she changed her dress, she concentrated on the encounter with Zig. The initial shock of his likeness to Edmund faded a bit. He was pleasant, a real gentleman, and she wanted to know more about him.

*There's no doubt in my mind he's Edmund's son. But how did he come to live with Martha?*

Maggie eyed the injured ankle as Phebe walked toward her. "Everything all right?"

"Yes, thanks. I'll hold onto the rail and follow you down. The ankle doesn't hurt, but it does feel a bit weak."

Dinner was set up in a large glassed-in porch. Even though it was almost six o'clock, the room was bathed in a soft, warm light from the setting sun. Mr. and Mrs. Powell sat at the end of a long table. The children occupied one side. She didn't see Zig.

Mr. Powell rose to pull out a chair for her, opposite the children. "There you are, Phebe. Elizabet told us about your unfortunate accident. I hope it isn't serious."

"Oh, not at all. It's fine now. I was a bit clumsy I fear."

Mrs. Powell leaned forward and patted her hand. "That's good to hear, my dear. You must take it easy for the rest of the visit. Are you sure you shouldn't see a doctor?"

"No, no need for a doctor. Elizabet did a proper job of wrapping it down by the lake. Kept the swelling down. Really, it was simply a tweak. I wouldn't say it was twisted."

"Nevertheless, I order you to rest. No more wandering

about for the rest of the trip." Mrs. Powell withdrew her hand and smiled.

"As you say, Mrs. Powell. My mouth is watering at the wonderful aroma drifting into the room. Where are Martha and, uh, Zig?"

Martha swept into the room carrying a large tray. "Here we are, my lovelies. My famous pot roast."

Maggie came behind carrying a soup tureen.

"Oh my, it smells heavenly. I'm starved." Phebe smiled at her host.

"I imagine you are after an afternoon by the lake." Martha set the tray in the middle of the table. "Robert, you may begin."

As Mr. Powell took each plate and filled it, Maggie dipped the ladle into the soup bowls. A lovely loaf of sourdough bread was sliced and ready to butter.

The group chatted merrily as they ate, but Phebe noticed Zig was not among the dinner guests.

Naturally, unable to squelch her curiosity, she posed the question. "May I ask where *Zig* is? He mentioned he would make it for dinner."

Martha smiled at her. "He came up with a great idea for the novel he's working on. Said he must get it down before it left him. I'll send him a plate later."

The pang of disappointment seared through her heart. Why his absence caused such a reaction surprised her. His face, of course, was so like Edmund's it was astonishing, but his bearing and demeanor were more relaxed and jovial. She liked him and hoped she could talk more with him.

The sun set, darkening the windows and signaling the

end of the meal.

Martha led the group from the room. "Let's have our dessert on the veranda. It's lovely this time of evening."

As Maggie served the lemon cake and poured coffee, the conversation bounced around from horse riding, fishing, and the benefits of country living.

But, Phebe wasn't listening. Instead, she trained her eyes on a small beam of light piercing the trees in the distance. It was barely visible, but she saw it.

*It's the cabin. Where Zig is working.*

She wanted to take a lantern and walk through the woods, but she didn't move.

Finally, Martha stretched and yawned. "I fear Zig is fair starving out there. Knowing him, he doesn't even realize he's hungry." She turned to Maggie. "Help me clean up, dear. I need to pack a basket for him."

"I can help, Martha," Phebe said.

Before her host could answer, Mr. Powell interrupted. "You need to help prepare the children for bed, Phebe, *if* your ankle can handle it. It drains Emma's strength to deal with all three."

"Of course, right away, Mr. Powell."

Martha and Maggie disappeared into the sunroom.

Phebe gathered the children and headed upstairs.

An hour later, Benjamin, Charley, and Elizabet were tucked tightly into bed.

She was exhausted, but took a moment to stand at the window and study the light from the cabin.

*He's still awake. I'd love to know what he is writing about.*

The tiny beacon continued to intrigue her. All thoughts

of sleep vanished.

*How I want to talk with him again.*

Time passed as she kept vigil, hoping he might appear and beckon to her.

But he didn't.

As she was about to turn away, the light changed. It started to bob, coming closer.

Her heart beat faster.

*Could it be him?*

But disappointment stabbed at her as she made out the shadowy figures of Martha and Maggie emerging from the trees. Maggie carried a lantern, the light bouncing up and down as they walked along the uneven path.

Thankful the candle was already extinguished, she knew they couldn't see her and watched until the light disappeared around the back of the house.

She turned back to the trees. The pinpoint of light from the cabin still pierced the dark night.

*Zig Evans. Anthony McAdams. Which is it? Will I ever find out?*

## Chapter TWENTY-NINE

Breakfast consisted of biscuits and gravy along with bacon cooked to perfection. Martha presided over a wood burning stove stirring the simmering gravy and checking the biscuits.

"Ah, good morning Phebe. I trust you slept well." Martha's friendly smile warmed the room.

"Yes, very well, thank you." She surveyed the room. "Am I late for breakfast?"

"Oh no. The children ate earlier. Robert and Emma won't rise for another hour. Sit down, we'll have our morning meal together."

Phebe pulled out a chair, but hesitated. "May I help you?"

"No, no. It's finished. Just need to serve it up."

Martha set a plate of biscuits on the table and turned to retrieve the rest.

A large pitcher of orange juice graced the middle of the table.

Martha glanced at Phebe as she dished up the savory fare. "You may pour the juice if you like."

The biscuits, so light and flaky, melted in her mouth. The perfectly seasoned gravy was smooth and rich.

"The children tell me you are the best cook around these parts. I think they're right. This is wonderful."

"Why, thank you, Phebe. I love to cook. Taught by my mama when I was a small girl standing on a step stool trying to see what she was doing. I've always had a love for cooking."

"Well, I thought Myrtle was the best cook around, but I believe you beat even *her* in that area. I wish I could learn all your secrets. I'm afraid I'm not much in the kitchen. Teaching suits me much better."

The light in Martha's blue eyes faded. "Yes, Myrtle…"

Phebe pounced on Martha's hesitation. "So, you know her?"

"Why…yes. I know her."

"I ask because I mentioned her to Zig last night. He said he'd never met her. It's odd to me, I guess. You know, since you are Robert's sister."

Martha sighed. "Zig told me you are a curious one. Asking questions, making pointed remarks."

Phebe jumped to her feet. "Oh, Ms. Martha, I *am* sorry. I have a curious nature, for sure, but I didn't mean to overstep. It's just, well, there are so many secrets in the family. Even the children ask me questions, things I can't answer. Strange occurrences in the house, everyone so unwilling to talk about anything. I want to fit into this family. I'm getting older and would like to make sure I enjoy a bit of security. I love working for the Powell's. I *do* apologize."

Martha rose, as well. "No need to apologize. Would you like to take a walk in the garden?"

The sudden shift in conversation caught her off guard. "Why, yes, of course. I was hoping I could see it before I left."

"Come." Martha reached out a hand.

Gingerly, she wound her arm through Martha's, who tightened her grip and led her through the door.

The garden was lush, well-cared for, and very colorful. Flowers, greenery, vegetables, all kinds of things grew here.

Martha guided her down the rows. "The season is coming to an end, I'm afraid. Soon, the frost will claim the color. My sanctuary will settle into its night's sleep, and I will have to find another way to count the days."

Phebe noticed the wistful look in Martha's eyes. "But surely, there are things you can grow in the winter, as well."

"Yes, but there's nothing like the sun-warmed earth between your fingers to wash away sorrow."

"You talk as if someone died."

Martha didn't answer as they strolled along in silence.

A stone bench graced the end of the last row of roses.

"Let's sit for a bit, Phebe."

After several moments of quiet, Martha slipped her arm from hers. "If you truly want a place in this family you must know certain things. But, at the same time, there are things you simply cannot ask about. Do you understand?"

"Yes, ma'am."

"You won't see Zig for the rest of this visit. He's withdrawn, except for the children. They're the only ones who can prod a smile from him."

Phebe stared at her. "Is that my fault? I brought up the wrong subject, didn't I?"

Martha continued. "You didn't know. We don't blame you. I'm going to tell you what I think you already know. Maybe then you can put things to rest in your mind."

"You don't have to…"

Martha brushed her aside and blurted, "Elizabet is Zig's child."

Phebe held her breath. *Am I finally going to hear the truth?*

"You see, Zig married a local girl six years ago. I didn't approve the marriage, but he was determined. I never could tell him no. We had a small ceremony here, in the garden. Robert and Emma came." Martha paused, staring into space.

Phebe whispered, "What happened?"

"They were about to welcome their first child into the world. Clara, Zig's wife, came down with a terrible cold. It worsened. She couldn't shake it. The doctors tried everything. Elizabet came early. Clara died in child birth."

"I'm so sorry," Phebe said.

"Yes, it was a hard time. Zig lost all interest in everything. Started brooding. Blamed himself. Said he should never have married her at such a young age. I cared for the baby because Zig couldn't even look at her for a time. He suffered such guilt. Eventually, he came out of it some, but he still has bouts of melancholy."

"I surmise your brother took her to raise?"

"Yes, it was Emma's idea. She had the two boys and

wanted a girl so much. Her boys drained her of strength. Robert didn't want her to try again. When they saw how much Zig suffered, they made the offer and Emma got her little girl."

Phebe asked another question. "But, Elizabet doesn't know?"

"No. It isn't the right time to tell her. She loves him so, but only knows him as uncle."

"But, she *will* figure it out, eventually. One only has to look at their eyes to see it."

"Yes," Martha whispered.

Silence settled over the two women. They sat together holding hands.

Phebe was reluctant to break the quiet contemplation, but wanted so much to ask about Edmund.

She didn't.

It took a lot for Martha to tell her this much, she dare not push it.

"Well, I have told you about Elizabet. I trust you'll keep our little secret for now. Zig is the one who must tell her. And Emma, of course. It is up to them as to when."

"Of course. I won't say a word. I do apologize for my curiosity. It won't happen again."

Martha stood. "Time to get back. Emma and Robert will want their breakfast. Why don't you come in and have a cup of coffee with me while I prepare the biscuits?"

Together, they strolled the path to the house.

To learn about Zig and Elizabet exceeded her expectations, but Martha didn't mention anything about Edmund or the possibility Zig was his son. The opportunity presented itself, for sure, but slipped away when Martha declared secrets were best kept hidden. And so, one mystery was solved, but two questions still burned in her soul. Who killed Edmund? And could she find proof Zig is Edmund's son?

The kitchen was empty when they arrived, and Martha hurried to the stove to prepare fresh biscuits. "Please, pour us each a cup of coffee. Sit and keep me company. The boys are walking the horses, and the girls are fishing with Zig. You can tell me about yourself."

Through the course of the morning, the Powell's ate breakfast, the boys returned, dirty and disheveled, and Phebe helped clean up the kitchen.

The day passed pleasantly.

The girls returned late that afternoon, full of stories of the fish they caught. A pang of disappointment shivered through her. She hoped to see Zig again, but her unbridled curiosity ruined any chance of that.

The next day, they rose early for the trip home. Hugs and smooches abounded between the children and Martha. Everyone said goodbye and the long trip home was underway.

She attempted one look back, hoping to see Zig emerge from the trees.

He did not.

# Chapter THIRTY

THE TRIP WAS OVER. PHEBE STRUGGLED TO PUT ZIG, out of her mind. Not so easy when each time she looked at Elizabet—*his* face appeared.

Martha's warning was clear. No more questions. Leave the family secrets to the family.

However, there was the matter of the disarray in the sky-parlor she discovered before leaving for Aunt Martha's. Whoever cleaned Mary's room on a regular basis might discover her if she went back upstairs. On the other hand, those books lying on the floor meant Edmund was back. She must find out for sure.

Exhausted from the trip home, it proved difficult to stay awake, so she paced until the house grew quiet.

At half past midnight, she tip-toed up the third-floor stairs.

The door to the parlor opened with only a touch. She gasped at the scene before her. The floor was empty, not one book out of place.

*Someone has been here. I know it couldn't be Edmund. He throws books. He never picks them up.*

The room appeared freshly dusted, everything in order, even the wine carafe and sherry glasses. Where there were five before, now six completed the circle, each gleamed as if newly washed.

Chills danced down her spine. *Who could have done this?* She stepped forward to examine the bookshelf. As she reached out, a vibration rumbled under her feet. She snatched her hand back, but the pulsation spread throughout the room.

*He's coming back.*

The room filled with light. In the brightness Edmund appeared.

"I hoped you would come," she whispered.

"Where have you been?" Edmund asked with a frown. "I came twice, but you never appeared."

"To the country with the children. I discovered something there…"

He waved her words aside. "Someone was here. I saw them."

"Someone? Who?"

"Winston. My trusted friend."

Phebe whispered, "Winston?"

"He cleaned the room. Returned the missing sherry glass."

"Did he see you?" she asked.

"No, I don't think so. I spoke to him, touched his shoulder, but he didn't respond."

She paced to the window and back. "Why would he

come up here to clean this room after all these years? Makes no sense."

"Look at this." Edmund stood by the side table and pointed to the wine carafe.

Phebe joined him, picked up the glass, and held it to the light. "The sixth glass doesn't match."

Edmund frowned. "What do you make of it?"

Phebe turned. "I'm not sure. We know someone is cleaning Mary's room. Whoever it is never touched the parlor until now. Makes no sense. Could it be two different people? Why would Winston clean the rooms?"

"I don't know what to think. I've never seen him up here before."

"It's something to ponder." She returned the wineglass to the mirrored tray. "I have other news, Edmund."

He only stared at the wineglass.

Phebe persisted, "I found your son."

His eyes blazed with light. "My..."

"Yes, Anthony."

"My son," he whispered.

"Yes, he lives with Mr. Powell's sister, Martha. She raised him. I only say it with confidence because Martha admitted Elizabet is Anthony's daughter. Confirmation he is your son, since you already know Elizabet is your granddaughter."

So, you've found him. I want to see my son."

"I'll try to make that happen. He doesn't remember this house. Says he's never been here. It might be difficult."

"I'm forever grateful for what you've found. Mary and I are together in the afterlife. We've found Elizabet. The only thing left is to see Anthony."

She searched Edmund's face. "We still must find out who murdered you. Don't forget that. By the way, the emerald ring. Did you give it to Winston?"

His eyebrows knit together as he stroked his chin. "Father gave it to me." He glanced at his hand. "It's gone. I don't remember."

"I found him wearing it. His anger was very apparent when I commented on it," Phebe said.

Edmund tried to reply, but faded from the room. In a flash he was gone.

"He's gone again." The room lost its warmth. She shivered.

---

At breakfast, Phebe watched Winston closely. He acted as always, stalwart, proper, disagreeable. Nothing out of the ordinary.

Myrtle bustled around the kitchen serving up the morning fare like she'd done for decades.

Conversation didn't flow on this morning. She wanted to ask Winston about the sky-parlor but couldn't give herself away. She wondered if Myrtle knew about his activity on the third floor.

More and more, the clues simply didn't add up. *Why does Winston suddenly care about the state of the sky-parlor?*

Time was of the essence. She must return the library key to Mrs. Powell. The children would find it odd if she was late to the classroom.

"Excuse me, my friends. Duty calls."

Winston nodded.

Myrtle watched her as she headed for the door to the main hall. "The classroom is through the other door. Have you forgotten?"

"Why no, I need to return the library key."

"They've already left for town. Mrs. Powell needs a new dress. Won't be back for a few hours. I can give it to them if you like."

"No, I think I'll choose another book to read. I'll see them when they get back. Thanks anyway." Phebe opened the door and slipped through.

Her intention wasn't to get another book, but to study the portrait of Lucy McAdams. *What happened to Jonathan's second wife after he died?*

The sudden slam of the door made her jump. She whirled around.

"Winston. What on earth?"

The signature frown was deeper than ever. "The children are waiting."

Locating Lucy would have to wait. "Of course. I'm coming."

---

The children showed quite a lot of spirit, which added to her distraction. Elizabet clung to her wanting all her attention. When class was over, Emma Powell called for the children. There was a birthday party they needed to attend.

Free of her duties for the night, she excused herself

from dinner and went to her room.

The irony to all this mystery was she wanted it solved and yet, she didn't. The visits with Edmund were pleasant, although sometimes, a little too otherworldly. He was a nice, kind man. The sort of man she would someday like to meet and maybe marry. But…that was not to be in her future. She was a spinster. Too old to find a suitable husband. And a ghost who loved another wasn't exactly a match made in heaven. Edmund and Mary are together. She took satisfaction in that.

The evening passed. The children came home. She tucked them into bed after hearing all three accounts of the party.

True to form, Cook arrived with a sandwich, scolded her for missing supper, and left. The warm bread made her sleepy, and she drifted off.

She woke with a start. *Eleven-thirty! Edmund will be coming.*

But, he didn't.

She waited to no avail, alone in the upper room.

The room closed in on her, suffocating, like a jail cell. She went to the window. The barn beckoned her. *The horses will calm me. I need to get out of the house.*

When her heart pulled in one direction, she seldom thought of the consequences. After stopping for a cloak, she hurried downstairs and out of the door.

The barn door opened easily, but she drew back at the sound of a carriage approaching. "Who in the world would come here this time of night?"

She was about to duck inside the barn when a voice

called out.

"Phebe, please wait."

She recognized the voice instantly. "Zig?"

"Yes, please. I need to talk with you. Thank God you're here."

"But, it's so late, Zig. What...?"

He stepped down from the carriage. "Mother and I got into an argument after you left. I was looking for the family bible. I needed a quote for my book. I found a paper enclosed inside. A family tree of sorts. *I* wasn't on it, but she was. I asked about it, but she refused to explain it. I've asked before about my father, she won't tell me anything. She implied you might have some answers."

"It's not my place, Zig. Need I remind you? You made it perfectly clear."

He took her hand. "You know *something*, Phebe."

The feel of his strong hand filled her with wonder. It was warm, but gentle. She closed her eyes, lost in the sensation. "Yes, I know."

"Then, tell me. What is going on?"

His eyes searched hers until she couldn't resist. "Follow me. I have something to show you."

The path to the cemetery was dark, but the bright moon gave them just enough light to make their way.

"A cemetery?" he asked.

"Yes, I want to show you, so you can see the truth." She pulled him harder as they made their way.

In the back corner, she stopped and pointed to Edmund's grave stone. "This is your father."

He moved to her side. "Edmund McAdams? But,

how…my last name is Evans."

"No Zig, it's not. It's McAdams. You're Anthony Maurice McAdams."

"I don't understand."

Phebe opened her mouth to answer, but stopped as a new shadow emerged from the trees.

"You!"

## Chapter THIRTY-ONE

This new intruder spat at Phebe, "I thought you might come here again. Can't keep your nose out of things, can you?"

"But, I...."

"What *are* we going to do about your morbid curiosity?"

"Whatever do you mean?"

"The way you can't leave the dead in peace. I'll have to tell Mr. Powell about this, you know. I fear your employment is about to come to an end. At the very least, a stern reprimand."

"I'm free to walk the grounds," Phebe said.

"But you're *not* free to wander to the third floor of the main house."

Phebe gasped. "It was you!"

Zig stepped in front of her. "Now see here…"

A knife gleamed in the moonlight. "You're a trespasser. You don't belong here. I'd have just cause—"

Phebe searched for a route of escape to no avail. *Only one card left to play.* "I know about Elizabet. Martha told me. It's only a matter of time before they tell her and when they do, the ugly truth about Edmund's death will be exposed."

Shock silenced her adversary, eyes wide, mouth open.

Phebe took advantage. "It *was* you, wasn't it? You killed Edmund."

The ground vibrated, a silvery light pulsated, elevating an ear-piercing noise.

"Edmund," she shouted.

"Yes, Phebe. I'm here."

"I know who killed you."

His green eyes glowed at the announcement, "Who is it then?"

Phebe pointed toward the knife-wielding intruder. "There."

Like a whirlwind, Edmund moved forward, engulfing the accused in the vortex of cold wind and gray fog. "I trusted you. Why did you take me from Mary?" he bellowed.

The intruder screamed. "What's happening, what is that light? The wind, I can't stand up!"

Phebe interceded. "Stop Edmund. We must hear the confession."

Zig stepped to her side. "She's right, we need to hear it all."

The whirlwind stopped. The noise subsided.

The killer cowered, face hidden behind shaking hands.

Edmund stepped toward Zig. "You can see me? Are

you... my son?"

Zig smiled. "Yes, I've only now come to learn who *you* are."

The ghost and the man regarded one another.

Edmund spoke softly, "I never knew about you while I was alive. It's only in death that your mother, Mary, encouraged me to find the truth."

Zig nodded, "I'm glad she did. *I* need answers, as well."

"Yes, but first, I must deal with my murderer." He turned his wrath on the cowering killer. "I need to know why," Edmund said. "My life—taken from me, from my Mary." He moved closer. "I trusted you. Loved you. How could you...?"

"Answer him. He deserves to know who killed him and why," Phebe demanded.

"Answer who?" The murderer pointed to Zig. "That man? He's nothing to me."

Phebe glanced toward the ghost. "You don't see Edmund? He's here to find out why you murdered him so mercilessly."

"Here? I don't see him." The confessor spun around. "It was a mistake! *Edmund* wasn't supposed to die."

Phebe gasped, "What? Then who were you after?"

White-faced, eyes round with terror, the voice lowered, barely audible. "It was supposed to be Mary."

Phebe glanced at Edmund.

Amber shards of light from his angry eyes shot toward the huddled mass in the corner. "Mary? You wanted to kill Mary?"

"You don't understand. I had no choice. Edmund wasn't

supposed to marry *her*. He was supposed to marry Lucy."

"Lucy? But…?"

The fright left the assassin's eyes, replaced with a steely resolve. "I worked hard to groom her. She was to have all the things I couldn't. *She* would be a lady."

Edmund shook his head. "She was a handmaid. *Mary's* handmaid. Lucy was a lovely girl, to say the least, but my heart belonged to Mary."

Phebe voice raised, "Mary was pregnant with Edmund's child when you murdered him." She turned to Zig. "This is Edmund's son. This is Anthony."

"I didn't know," the killer trembled.

The vibration resumed, and Edmund's wrath cast the dark cemetery into an eerie purple light with swirling wind, fog, and a terrible cold.

Phebe tried to calm him.

The deranged killer wielded the knife high in the air. "I've kept the secret all these years. I've tried to atone, but now, I must end it."

"No! Stop. I've brought the constable and his officer." Jake's frightened voice pierced through the night air.

Zig sprung forward and wrestled the knife away.

"Hold her there," Phebe said. "You're going to confess. Anthony deserves to know the despicable things you've done. I thought you were my friend, too. Turns out you're just a pathetic soul with no conscience."

The constable stepped forward. "Someone want to tell me what's going on here?"

"Arrest this woman for murder," Phebe demanded.

"Arrest Myrtle? What murder?"

"*Murders*, Constable. She killed Edmund McAdams, as well as Mary McAdams."

---

The constable's carriage rambled down the road toward town carrying Myrtle Godwin with him. One officer stayed behind.

Phebe, Jake, and Zig remained in the damp cemetery, shaken with disbelief.

"We must tell them. Mr. and Mrs. Powell. How will they ever believe it?" Phebe asked.

"A difficult task, but it must be done," Zig declared.

She turned to Jake. "How did you know to get the constable?"

"I saw the light. It was brighter than usual. I climbed out the window—saw shadows around the graves, heard angry voices. Constable doesn't live far from here. I ran as fast as I could."

"Wait, where's Edmund?" Phebe asked. "He's gone."

The light strengthened from the shadows. "No, I'm here."

"It's over Edmund. You've met your son. We know who killed you, and why."

"Not quite. I know Jonathan is dead, but where's Lucy? There's no gravestone for her," Edmund declared.

## Chapter
# THIRTY-TWO

Edmund's question hung in the damp air.

Phebe turned to the stone markers barely visible in the swirling fog. "Jonathan is buried next to Mary." She peered into the darkness. "Where *is* Lucy?"

"*Who* is Lucy?" Zig asked.

Phebe smiled. "That's right, you don't know. Lucy is Myrtle's sister. She was also Jonathan's second wife."

"Jonathan?"

"Edmund's brother."

"A brother?" Zig pressed. "I don't quite understand. My mother married Jonathan after my father's death?"

Phebe nodded. "Yes."

"Because of me? She was already with child." He pointed to Edmund. "His child? Not Jonathan's."

"Yes. It would've ruined Mary completely. Jonathan gave you a proper name. Kept everything respectable. He'd always wanted Mary for himself. When you were two years old, Jonathan and Mary had a daughter. Emma. Mary died, or as we now know, was murdered shortly after her birth. Jonathan married Lucy. But, I don't see her grave anywhere."

"Could she still be alive?" Zig asked.

The ghostly light dimmed, deepening the blackness of the night.

She clutched the wool cloak tighter. "It's cold. We need to get home, tell the household. We'll have to find Lucy later." She looked around. "Edmund, I…"

The ghost faded, but a smile danced in his bright eyes as Mary stood beside him.

"Look Zig, they're together," Phebe said.

"I see," he replied. "Isn't Mother beautiful?"

Misty eyes blurred her vision. "Mary's never appeared before. They can rest in peace, now. Together."

Zig's strong hands grasped hers. "But now, there is more to finish."

"Yes," she said.

Jake tugged at her cloak. "I see them, too, Phebe. Both of them. They're leaving."

Zig and Phebe turned to see Edmund and Mary fade into the darkness, arms around each other. Edmund's green eyes filled with love, the amber shards now golden flecks.

They watched until Edmund and Mary dissolved into the mist.

"Come," Phebe whispered. "We need to explain to the Powell's."

The three walked together toward the big house. Each with their own thoughts on how Myrtle's confession changed everything.

"What do you mean waking the house before dawn, Phebe?" Mr. Powell asked. "What couldn't wait until morning? What is Zig doing here?"

"I'm sorry, truly, but there's been an arrest," she answered.

"An arrest? Who?" Mr. Powell glanced around the room.

"It's Myrtle."

"Myrtle? You mean Cook?" he asked. "Arrested for what?"

"Murder."

Mrs. Powell gasped.

The night in the cemetery, Myrtle's confession, the distasteful task of informing the Powell's. Well, it was unbearable. Zig and Jack stood by her as the explanation ensued.

The Powell's stood white-faced.

Winston's on guard demeanor cracked and real fear shone in his eyes.

"The constable is coming soon to confirm what I've told you. I'll make some coffee. We can gather in the kitchen where it's warm." She looked at the butler. "There's a guard outside. The constable will want to question you, as well."

Winston gave his curt nod, but his shoulders sagged, and his former straight-laced bearing evaporated.

As day broke, the constable arrived and confirmed the truth.

He also produced a signed document by Myrtle. There *was* a will. She and Winston hid it after the deaths of

Edmund's parents. Everything was left to Edmund and his heirs. In fact, Jonathan was a product of a secret affair by Edmund's father. It was all there, in the confession. He convinced his lover to let him raise the boy. Paid her a handsome sum to disappear, but Jonathan was never added to the will.

Edmund and his heirs remain the sole recipients of the property. Emma Powell's claim was invalid.

"It's so much to take in. This house belongs to Zig and Elizabet," she whispered.

Emma Powell wept as the constable read the will, found where Myrtle said it would be. Mr. Powell strutted like a peacock disputing its authenticity, spouting he would sue.

While Mr. Powell continued to sputter and protest, Phebe drew the constable to the side. "Does anyone know of Lucy's whereabouts? Is she dead?"

The constable whispered, "Myrtle told me she's alive."

Phebe gasped. "But where?"

The constable turned to the butler. "Winston, the jig is up, sir. Will you lead the way?"

Winston stood by the door.

*There is resignation in his eyes. He knows the ugly truth will reach its bony fingers toward him.*

The constable called for silence. "Winston? I'm waiting."

The aging butler gazed at Phebe.

She expected to see hatred in his eyes, but all she saw was defeat.

He muttered, "She's upstairs—on the third floor."

Phebe and Zig followed the others upstairs.

They found her not in Mary's room, but in a smaller one farther down the hall.

Disheveled, rocking in her chair, she talked nothing but gibberish. When she saw Winston, her eyes lit up. "Sister. Where is sister?"

He bent to her, smoothing her unkempt hair. "Sister had to go away, dear. And so do you. This nice man will take you to a new place. You'll have a lovely room, people to care for you."

"No, want sister!"

"I know best, remember? Things will turn out fine. You trust me, don't you?"

She nodded.

The constable took her arm and gently pulled her up. "Come now, we'll go for a nice ride in the fresh air. Won't that be nice?"

Lucy looked at Winston who gave her a rare smile as he took her other arm and led her from the room.

Phebe watched them go. "How did I not know she was up here. I came often to see Edmund. I even went into Mary's room next door. I never once suspected someone else lived up here."

"They've hidden her for years. She must know the truth about the murders. Maybe they were afraid she would tell," Zig said.

"Winston will go to jail, too, won't he?" Phebe asked.

"He's a conspirator. I'm afraid he will."

Phebe and Zig went to the sky-parlor and watched through the window while the constable helped Lucy into the wagon. Winston climbed in beside her.

"I wonder if I will ever see them again?" she whispered.

---

Zig gave the Powell's ample time to vacate Queens Court Acres. They moved their personal belongings to Martha's until they could decide their next move.

Phebe remained the governess for as long as they took to move out, carrying out her duties to all three children.

Robert Powell's blustering subsided over the next two weeks when he realized nothing was in his favor.

When the day arrived and the last of their belongings was loaded on the carriage, Zig stood in the doorway with his hand clasped with Elizabet's. "She's my daughter. I should never have let her go. She'll live in this house with me, where she belongs."

Mrs. Powell wept silently in the back of the carriage.

Mr. Powell said nothing, just turned on his heel and took his place beside his wife.

Phebe hung back inside the foyer. When the Powell's disappeared, she turned and went upstairs to pack.

The mystery was solved. Justice was done.

*There's no need for me to stay. Elizabet has her father, now.*

Before she hauled the heavy suitcase downstairs, she made the last trip to the sky-parlor. The emptiness of the room saddened her. She'd never see Edmund again, but it was enough to know she helped find him peace.

As she turned, a shadow darkened the doorway.

"Phebe, where are you going? Your suitcase is in the hallway."

It was Zig. The amber shards in his green eyes shining as daylight poured through the window.

"No need for me to stay. The Powell's don't want me after I've single-handedly destroyed their lives here. I'll go home to my family. Find another position."

"But, what about me—and Elizabet?" he asked.

She smiled. "You have each other. You'll be fine."

He took her hands. "No, no we won't. Not without you. We want you to stay.

She looked down at his strong, warm hands. "I can't… why Zig, where did you get Edmund's ring?

The emerald ring she first saw in Edmund's portrait sparkled on Zig's hand. To her, it represented a happy Edmund, when he was in love with Mary.

"It's Edmund's. Winston slipped it to me as he helped Lucy out the door. He whispered in my ear. "You should have this. It's your father's."

"Oh, my goodness. It's come full circle. I'm so pleased for you, Zig.

"No, not everything is complete, Phebe. There's one more thing." He bent to one knee. "Everyone should be with the one they love, and I love you. Will you marry me and complete the circle?"

"But, Zig, I can't …"

"Phebe, you risked your employment to hunt for the truth; you were the one who Elizabet bonded with; you helped set Edmund free; *you* risked your life to expose the treachery of Winston and Myrtle; your curiosity brought our family back to life…even the sun brightens when I speak your name. Please, be my wife."

The sky-parlor glowed with the light of a benevolent sun.

Phebe's heart swelled as he kissed her hand while she gathered the courage to answer what she wanted to scream to the world. Instead, she whispered, "Yes, Zig, yes. I'll marry you."

THE END

# Acknowledgements

My husband is first on my list for the support he gives me in my writing career. I could never follow my dream without him.

Many thanks to my critique partner, Nancy Hudgins, for her great ability to spot my weaknesses and bring them to my attention.

Also, thanks to Ruth Buck, my proof reader. Her eagle eyes pick up any frailties in my manuscripts and sets me back on track.

To all the many people behind the scenes who push me forward and keep me going. Thank you!

# About the Author

Award Winning Author Patty Wiseman is a native of the Seattle, Washington area and attended The Wesleyan College in Bartlesville, Oklahoma. Northeast Texas is home, now, along with her husband Ron. She created the Vintage Mystery Series, The Velvet Shoe Collection set in the 1920's. Intrigue with a touch of romance fuel the stories of strong women who overcome obstacles and propel them into strength and triumph.

Her books include: *An Unlikely Arrangement*—won 2nd place in Forward National Literature Awards, *An Unlikely Beginning*, won 1st place in Texas Association of Authors in Romance, *An Unlikely Conclusion*—won 1st place in Texas Association of Authors in Romance, a brand new book,

*An Unlikely Deception*—Book Four of the series, and a contemporary romance titled *That One Moment*. She's also written a motivational book called *Success Your Way— Make a Wish, then Make a Plan*.

She is the President of the East Texas Writers Association, member of Texas Federation of Women's Clubs—Marshall Chapter, a Lifetime Member of the Worldwide Who's Who for Professional Women, named VIP for 2013, the Northeast Texas Writer's Organization, East Texas Writers Guild and Texas Association of Authors

Favorite quote "Find out who you are, then do it on purpose." ~ Dolly Parton

Website: www.pattywiseman.com

Facebook: www.facebook.com/PattyWisemanAuthor

Twitter: twitter.com/PattyWG

Email: patty_wiseman1966@yahoo.com

GooglePlus: plus.google.com/+PattyWisemanAuthor

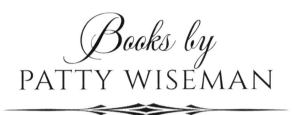

### The Velvet Shoe Collection

*An Unlikely Arrangement*
*An Unlikely Beginning*
*An Unlikely Conclusion*
*An Unlikely Deception*

*Success Your Way*

*That One Moment*

*Rescue At Wiseman's Pond*

*Somewhere Between*

*Preview of*

# CHAPTER One

Ricki Sheridan didn't expect to die falling off a mountain ledge.

One misstep, a soft spot on the trail, and her leather hiking boot slipped over the edge, sending a shower of gravel over the jagged cliff.

Unbalanced and top-heavy, her scream echoed across the deep ravine like a wounded loon falling from the sky. She jerked the backpack to the right, dragged her left foot up the ridge, and fell against the rocky cliff gasping for air.

A misty fog wet her face and chilled her fingers while tendrils of fear snaked around every nerve. *Breathe, Ricki, you didn't go over. You're okay.*

She shrugged the pack off her shoulder and eased her already sore body onto the makeshift cushion. The trembling persisted, uncontrolled and violent.

*Crap, a little too close for comfort.*

Thankful no one witnessed the near disaster, she gulped the crisp mountain air to restore balance and quiet the pounding in her chest. A mixture of grit and sweat slid over one brow and stung her eye. The only thing available to erase the grime and unbidden tears was the sleeve of her faded denim shirt, which she hastily swiped across her face.

The pup tent on top of the pack slid to one side. She stood to re-center it, and mumbled, "This trip might be a bad idea. I should have stayed in Texas."

A devastating betrayal found her on this mountain to help eradicate the pain from her mind. Ricki is a strong woman most times, but the most vulnerable aspect of her personality failed her, again. When it comes to men, she always chooses the wrong one. This time was the last straw, because *this time* it involved her best friend.

Another deep breath diminished the shaking. "Lucky I didn't tumble down on top of the *second* team."

"You all right?"

A deep male voice made her jump and spin around. Off balance again, she teetered to the right and kicked another spray of gravel over the edge.

The man reached out to steady her. "Whoa, let me help you."

He was one of the trail bosses. She saw him at Wolf's Den Lodge, noticed his ink black eyes and quick smile, but chose to hang back and keep her distance. When the group took to the trail, she decided to bring up the rear. As a result, she fell farther behind the others, but it suited her purpose. Her goal was to be alone. She aimed to keep it that way.

"Thanks, I'm fine, just tripped. Pack is a little off balance. I've got it covered."

Her wanna-be rescuer ran a hand through thick, raven hair, assessed her with a glance, and said softly. "You look like you need a break."

Overcome with a sudden awareness of her physical state, her hand went swiftly to her own disheveled mane. She smoothed the windblown tangles as best she could. "I said I could handle it. It's steep here, that's all. I was looking up instead of at the trail. No harm done."

"What's your name?"

She ducked her head. "Ricki Sheridan."

He stretched out his hand. "We didn't get to meet formally. I'm Kory Littleton, Trail Boss."

"I know who you are." The rude retort wasn't natural to her, but necessary to keep the distance she coveted.

"I saw your name on the list. Nice to put a face to it. Ever been on a pack trip before? This is a good mountain to start on."

To her relief, she didn't have a chance to answer. Another group arrived in single file, impatient, and unable to pass.

A short, scruffy man scanned the sky and looked back at Kory. "You gonna stop on this narrow ledge or what, Chief? It'll be nightfall soon."

Shadows darkened the snow tipped peaks, clouds drifted across the late afternoon sky, and a keen breeze cut through Ricki's thin shirt.

She shivered.

Littleton stepped around in front. "Take your troop on ahead. The lady experienced a small set-back. Her ankle's bleeding. I'm gonna doctor it." He lowered his voice.

"Watch the trail over there, Steve, it's soft. Don't want anyone to slip off the mountain."

Steve Gorman eyed the edge of the trail and turned back to survey Ricki's injured ankle. He nodded and spit a stream of tobacco juice into the dirt.

She looked down. Blood oozed over the thick, woolen sock onto her low rider boot.

"Next time, try the high-tops. They're safer," Steve said. He brushed by, motioning the others to follow. He and the rest of his band followed him around the bend.

"Sit down, the first aid kit is in my pack," Kory ordered.

Her chin rose in defiance, another chink in her armor—a quick temper. "Thanks, I can bandage it. Take care of the rest of your group."

He grinned good-naturedly and displayed a cheerful salute. "I'm an Eagles Pass Trail Boss, ma'am. We never leave anyone behind. It's our motto. I'm the head guide, gotta set the example." The bulky pack slipped easily off his broad back.

"Head guide, huh? What makes you so special?" Embarrassed about her clumsy mishap, she couldn't resist the urge to goad him.

"Oh, I don't know, probably because I've been around longer—saved a few more lives." The smile flashed again before his teeth ripped through the adhesive bandage. "Now hold still, I've done this a couple of million times, we'll be through in a flash."

She flinched at his touch as a small shock of pain raced through the ankle.

"It's bruised, and it'll be tender, but should be fine," he said.

She watched his face as he worked. The image of trail boss conjured up flannel shirts, knee-high boots, a gruff personality, and five o'clock shadow. *This one is different. Clean shaven, strong white teeth, weathered skin, and he's kind. He's got the red flannel shirt down, though.*

She shivered again, this time from his strong hand holding her ankle so gently. "Look, Mr. Littleton, I appreciate your help. The backpack got the better of me, I admit… packed too heavy. I'll fix it and be right along. Please get back to the others. I'm an experienced back-packer, thanks to my father. I know the mountains."

"The *name* is Kory. Steve is my back up. We need to stick to the rules. I'll help you rearrange your load, and we'll both catch up. We don't leave anyone behind, remember? 'Fraid you're stuck with me. Can you put weight on the ankle?" He slung her pack over one shoulder and heaved his pack over the other arm.

She winced at his reprimand, but eased herself to a stand. "Yes, it's okay."

Taking orders wasn't her strong suit. From the ROTC program in high school and college to a Crime Scene Forensic Investigator in the U.S. Navy, she was used to having the upper hand. But, it was all over now. After her enlistment was up, she turned civilian and applied for the game warden academy. She was assigned to a position in Dallas after graduation. Wildlife suited her more than a stuffy office. She thrived in the outdoors with nothing to confine her but the blue sky.

"Better get a move on, then. There's a wide spot in the trail up ahead. We'll reorganize there." He disappeared around the bend.

She followed slowly, testing the ankle with each step.

Sprawled on a rotten log, he systematically unloaded the first few contents of her pack. The boyish grin flashed, again, as he held up a small journal. "Ah, reading material. Hope you don't plan to keep your nose in a book the whole time. This is a retreat, I know, but don't forget we have nine other people here. Good practice to interact with the other campers."

She snatched it from his hand. "Put it down. It's none of your business. I said *I'll* redo my pack."

Kory drew back his hand—the smile disappeared. "Sorry Ricki, I meant no harm. Chill out, I didn't peek."

She flung the remaining contents on the ground, one a time. "This trip's a big mistake. I'm heading back to the lodge."

His voice changed from jovial to real concern. "Hey, slow down. You'll never make it down the mountain before dark. The weather calls for a storm sometime tomorrow. I can't let you go." He picked up each item she threw at him and organized them according to weight and size.

She stomped her good foot. "You can't stop me. I paid my money. It's on *my* head. I don't want to do this anymore."

To her horror, hot tears trickled down her face. She started to shake.

In one stride, he reached her before she toppled over. "I apologize, Ricki. Sit down. You're exhausted. Six miles is a lot when it's uphill luggin' a pack, especially if you haven't done it in a while. I'm here for a reason, let me do my job."

Suddenly, weakness overcame her in a most disconcerting way. She collapsed against him, sobs wracking her body.

His strong arms encircled her. He wiped two large tears from her cheek with his thumb, and whispered softly, "It's okay, Freckles. We all have our breaking point."

"Don't call me Freckles!" She gulped between sobs, the unpredictable temper blazed hot.

"I'm sorry—again. I can't say anything right, it seems. Too long in the mountains, I guess." He hesitated. "I meant it as a compliment. They're very pretty on you."

"I…I never cry. Never." The temper subsided into annoyance.

He held her a little too tight and whispered a little too softly in her ear, "Maybe it's time to let go."

The sobs stopped abruptly at the intimate encounter. She pulled away and wiped her eyes on one dirty sleeve. "It's over now. It won't happen again."

He turned, grabbed a bedroll, and spread it on the ground. "Sit." His voice left no room for argument.

Never in her memory had she done anything so embarrassing, so out of character. Self-control was one of her strong suits, a source of pride to her. Military training taught her well.

He rearranged each item in her pack, buckled it up, re-cinched the straps, and set it against the dead log. "All finished. Feelin' any better?" He squatted on his heels in front of her. "You're in no shape to hike down the mountain.

Let's see if we can sort this out before we rejoin the others."

Her protest withered on quivering lips. Voices echoed in the faded forest. Someone or some*thing* was about to round the bend.

*Available Now*

Made in the USA
Columbia, SC
29 November 2018